AM I MY BROTHER'S KEEPER?

Some secrets can't stay buried forever.

J.C. Benson

Jai Publishing House Incorporated
Promenade II
1230 Peachtree Street NE | 19th Floor
Atlanta, Georgia 30309
www.jaipublishing.com

Ordering Information: Quantity sales. Special discounts are available on quantity purchases by corporations, associations, and others. For details, contact the publisher at the address above.

Printed in the United States of America

ISBN-13: 978-1-7366613-4-5

I would like to dedicate this book to the village of loved ones who have greatly influenced my life and helped to cultivate the man that I am today.

Contents

LEFT BLANK INTENTIONALLY

"My mind is like a flower in bloom."

- Jay Z

LEFT BLANK INTENTIONALLY

AM I MY BROTHER'S KEEPER?

Some secrets can't stay buried forever.

J.C. Benson

Coming Home

J ameson Allen Clarkson sits back, eyes closed, he's tired. The show has been exhausting, almost as excruciating as it was a year ago.

Not as shocking, but heart-wrenching nonetheless. His normal stoic demeanor was not dominant today...

He rubs his eyes as his producer is in his ear for the last segment, "Five, four..." Jameson opens his eyes and pierces the room, but everyone has left.

"three... two... one..."

Jameson clears his throat slightly and slowly rubs his eyes with his hands...

"Todays' show has been difficult for obvious reasons. I genuinely believe we do help our audience on a day to day basis on this show. You allow us into your personal space, and as I always tell you, I will never take that for granted and I genuinely appreciate the sincerity that you have shown us. But honestly I feel like you've done that today for me."

He sighs, then continues, " The tragedy of losing Kobe Bryant a year ago today was painful and shocking. I have never felt those type of emotions for someone I never had a relationship with. As a black man, having these discussions, reading, listening and viewing others like myself, it felt like we lost a brother. I don't believe in most of our lifetimes we've lost someone with that broad of an audience so quickly and without warning.

So today we opened the show up and allowed everyone to express their feelings. Just get out what's on your mind. Not only men, but women, and young adults as well. I believe this has been a great vehicle for speaking in ways that few of us, especially black men are permitted to in public. I say 'permitted' because so many of us hold on to the public persona that is given to us. So, I do relish in the fact that this tragedy has allowed the masses to mourn, to show true feelings and be vulnerable."

Jameson scans the room. Over two years ago when he began his journey, the room intimidated him. He began his journey at a coffee shop scribbling notes on a napkin, then he upgraded to an 8x10-inch room with stale air and barely enough room for his small crew consisting of himself, a producer and an assistant to move without stepping on one another.

He recalls his voice not being loud enough when he first spoke into the microphone, the same microphone now that he towers over and is not only loud but powerful, confident, and eager to speak into. There were many nights early on when he and his producer would spend their last $5 on a Little Caesars pizza and drink water because that was all they could afford to eat.

He can still remember how the pizza would taste like that cardboard it sat in, yet they would eat every slice, enjoy the laughs and leave with a full stomach. The days when money was not plentiful but everyone stuck together for the love of what they were doing.

Jameson now stared at his wrist, where a black beaded bracelet hung off of his left wrist. He recalls being so happy when he was able to pull cash out of his pocket and not use an almost-maxed-out credit card to pay for it.

His stomach feels empty as he glances at the small heart tattoo still can be seen on his left index finger. A small symbol and only evidence of his short-lived marriage. The wedding was beautiful and fun, but its union was short-lived. A lesson that makes him feel empty and hollow, unfulfilled dreams and promises, families divided and lives that will never be the same.

The remainder of his outfit was very casual, gray jeans and a black V-neck t-shirt. Jameson would always remember this radio station for everything it represented from his past, present and now future. He would forever be indebted to the cobwebs, cold air drafts and terrible coffee in the break room, but would also remember that without the humble beginnings, there is no way he would appreciate what was to come.

Jameson continues...

"As a few of you may know, today is my last day here at WSRP. I appreciate the station in honoring our contract until the last date, that does not always happen in this industry," he says smirkily, then the smile disappears as he recounts, "They gave someone like myself, with a moniker The Doctor of Black Love, a chance when few would.

I started out doing this as a blog on my website, which turned into Facebook and Instagram live-streaming. That led to a late night spot on this station and eventually placed in the 3 to 7 p.m. time slot where we've stood strong for 2 years now.

Now I have been blessed with the opportunity to go home, like the Prodigal son from the Bible. However, thankfully I am not going home destitute or in need of anything. We have a great opportunity to build and grow from there. I will forever be appreciative of my humble beginnings and trust me, you haven't seen the last of me yet... in fact, you will be able to find me in the coming months.

As always remember... love only enters your heart if it is willing to receive it, signing off one last time... Dr. Black Love."

"That's a wrap Jameson, great job," Travis states as he begins to shut down the equipment and wrap up the session. The usual job for a producer, and he's worked with Jameson since day one —one of the best jobs he's ever had. Jameson is good people.

"Travis I appreciate it. I know I can be an asshole at times but I enjoyed working with you," Jameson jokingly shares his sentiment for a producer-turned-friend.

"Yeah you're an asshole but you're worth working with."

They give one another dap and Travis leaves. A text comes in.

Shelly: Great show sexy, you coming to see me tonight???

Me: I think so, going to see Zanita first

Shelly: or to see Camryn 🙄

No response.

Jameson packs his belongings and heads out of the studio. The place is pretty desolate, few staff are in since the pandemic hit. Many of them have been laid off actually. Landing his new contract was truly a blessing, social media is the great equalizer.

Outside the air is hot and thick, dark skies with a million stars above, Jameson never grew too fond of the triple digit dry summers in Phoenix. Where the air is just enough to make you bead sweat on your forehead, but never humid enough to make you sweat profusely.

The outline of the mountains that circled the entire valley were picturesque. They always looked to be so far away as the illusion of the desert would always play tricks with your mind. The clear skies would birth to beautiful and illustrious night falls almost daily.

There is an air of peace about his stride tonight, teetering on the edge of cockiness, his tall frame and broad shoulders stood out wider tonight. His beard was neatly trimmed and his hazel eyes had a glow to them. For many years, he shuffled around and about not knowing where he was going in the moment or in life. And then an idea popped in his head and he ran with it. Now, he had a clear plan and vision of what he was going to do.

A couple years ago he thought to himself, "There are a million shows with white people giving advice, shit I can give advice my damn self. I made enough mistakes, broke enough hearts, had mine broken as well... I can be honest and truthful as I have always been and build a market for us."

From that point on for the next year, if he wasn't taking care of his young daughter Zanita, he was working on Dr. Black Love.

First it was just a website with his friends and co-workers being his only followers. Initially, he treated his website as a *Dear Abby* copy cat. He answered questions sent in, sometimes they weren't even new but they were all his honest feedback about situations he had seen or experienced himself.

He had two rules... always be honest, and never embarrass anyone by giving their real names.

He had some small following but once he started posting live videos on Facebook and Instagram, he blew the hell up. It all led to a late night Friday evening only, short term contract on the radio. But he had to take the chance, he quit his 6-figure job and studied over and over what made media, marketing and the like work and never looked back.

Now he had positioned himself to negotiate a deal to get himself back home to Pittsburgh, given himself a hefty raise, he has a budget that will allow him to have a staff and freedom.

Jameson sits in his 2020 black Audi 6, he loves this car. It still smells and looks brand new. On his drive to his ex-wife's house, their old house, he doesn't take the highway, instead he drives the surface streets—as they call it in the desert.

All the windows are down, Jay Z's *Reasonable Doubt* plays in the background, just loud enough to sing along, but low enough to think when needed.

He drove these streets for nearly a decade, moving here knowing nobody but his ex, to building two successful careers. He never wanted to put roots here forever, he missed the East coast.

He stops in the driveway of his old home.

Many memories, some good, others are terrible.

Jameson's stomach always gets queasy when he hits the block. Generally he relieves the feeling by calling his ex-wife, Camryn, ahead of time to make sure Zanita is ready so that the exchange is swift. Tonight, however, he would have to walk inside—he's leaving tomorrow and his princess will be in the bed. The hardest part about this whole deal is having to say good-bye to Zanita.

He notices the front yard grass needs to be cut, the front door needs to be painted, and one of the front lights is out.

"I guess her in and out boyfriend don't give a shit about the house," he snarks. An incoming text breaks his thought, Jameson grabs his phone and unlocks the screen to read:

> Open the garage when you get here, I'm not getting up.

Camryn

He slams the phone down, and sighs to himself. Camryn never took any initiative unless it directly benefited her. This was the cause of many arguments, but he failed to see this flaw in her character until the end of their relationship.

He never regretted his daughter, but over the years he wondered what he actually saw in Camryn. At least he was leaving soon and would not have to deal with her selfishness. Jameson shuts off his car and gets out.

Jameson opens the garage, "Same damn code and I've been gone a year."

The smell of lavender permeates throughout the downstairs. He stops for a quick moment and recalls the good times they had. Dinners, parties, hanging out watching television.

At times when you are going through hell, it's hard to remember anything good especially when it comes to a marriage ending. Needless to say, he was appreciative of some things, but in a much more positive space now.

The house is very neat, well kept and actually looks better than when he left. Jameson walks upstairs and enters Zanita's bedroom.

There she is, Zanita Clarkson, the princess, the most beautiful 6-year-old the world has ever seen. She is peacefully sleeping, holding onto her pink blanket she has had since her first day on earth. Four pigtails neatly tied together with a pink bow fall to her shoulders.

He walks over and gently touches her on the shoulder, rubbing ever so gently as to not frighten her. With her eyes still closed she smiles.

"Sweetheart, sweetheart wake up," Jameson says softly. Zanita opens her eyes with excitement to see her Father.

"Hi Daddy, can I come with you?"

Jameson picks Zanita up, places her gently on his lap, and snuggles her into his arms.

"No baby, I wish you could, but Daddy has to get situated first. I don't even have a place to live yet, I have so much to do. And you have school to finish, you have friends here..."

Zanita's eyes begin to water.

"I know this is very hard... it's hard for you, Mommy and me. But I promise you, this will all make sense in the end. And you're coming to stay with Daddy for the entire summer. How's that sound? Sounds good?"

Zanita slowly nods while tears slowly build into her eyes. She puts her face in Jameson's shirt. His heart melts as he holds her.

Jameson still remembers first holding her when she was born. He was amazed that something so beautiful could come partly from him. He was deathly scared of being cursed with a daughter as his friends teased him about. Karma for being a man-whore and never committing to anyone outside of himself for too long.

But as he held Zanita only moments after she was born, they locked eyes and has been in love with her ever since. Their bond is undeniable, and love is unconditional. If nothing else in the world, Jameson knows he is an amazing father, that is the one job he can never and will never fail at, period.

Zanita still has her face buried in his shirt, anyone else in the world and they would be pushed back quickly from ruining one of his $250 shirts. But this little girl has him wrapped around her tiny, perfect fingers.

"Get some sleep princess. You can FaceTime me any time you want on your iPad, and I will be out here as often as I can before the summer. I promise."

"You promise?" Those big beautiful eyes looking up at her Daddy like he's the only king she needs. She believes every word he says.

"Absolutely."

Jameson lays Zanita back in her bed, tucks her in and hands her the pink blanket.

"Whose the most intelligent and beautiful 6-year-old black girl in the world?"

"Zanita Camilla Clarkson!"

"That's right my love," Jameson kisses Zanita on the forehead three times, sits next to her for a few moments until she falls back to sleep, and quietly leaves her room, closing the door behind him. Holding the door knob for a few seconds, he lets go and heads towards the steps.

Camryn opens the bedroom door and walks out.

"You're not going to come say good-bye?"

Jameson slows down and stops walking before responding. Over the years he has learned to tame his conversations with Camryn. Previously he allowed his initial reactions of annoyance and anger to boil over into every interaction with her. Now, he pauses, allows the emotion to die down inside before responding. It took some time to get into this space, and internally, Jameson was proud of his progress.

"Why would I do that Camryn?" Jameson answers coldly.

"Because not doing that would be rude considering you're leaving me and your daughter all out here by ourselves."

Jameson sighs... "You agreed to the plan, I don't like it, but this is the only way I can make it work, as we've discussed a number of times Camryn." Breathe, Jameson... breathe...

"Doesn't make it any easier," she barked. Rolling her eyes and crossing her arms. The audacity of this man to think he can run off and leave her to raise his kid.

"We have plenty of people out here that can help you, you know that. I'll get out here once a month, she's coming out for the summer, and then we'll figure it out from there."

"I might need help in the house," Camryn states bluntly.

"What the fuck does that mean?" But he already knew the answer, he just wanted her to say it.

"Antwan might move in..."

"Of course he will. You're gonna do what you want anyway..." Jameson starts to walk down the steps farther. Just a few steps away from the front door and back to his peaceful state. Eyes forward.

"That's all you have to say?" Camryn pushes the envelope. She knew him all too well. She knew the buttons and enjoyed pushing them every now and then. He's leaving, one more time for the road.

"For now... good night, Camryn." Jameson walks out of the house. With his back to Camryn who's watching him walk away, he smiles. *Not tonight.*

Shelly had always been good to him, but she was easy. Not easy in terms of not being intelligent but easy in terms of her situation. She was in her early forties, had three children so her time was limited, and he would only come over when her children were sleep, it was the classic lay-up as he often described on his show. Someone that can easily fulfill your needs but there would never be any long term commitment, or more importantly, any demands placed on your time.

Normally Jameson has a one track mind, especially with Shelly, and even more so when it comes to sex.

Shelly had an amazing body, especially for someone that had three children. She was classic 36-24-36, shaped exactly like a coke bottle, just like Jameson preferred. She stood at 5'11 inches, had long, thick brown hair, brown eyes, full lips, and always smelled like vanilla and strawberries, two of Jameson's favorite aromas from head to toe.

And on most nights, he loved nothing more than for her legs being pushed as high above her head as possible and for Jameson to slowly thrust in and outside of her until she couldn't take it, or him, anymore.

As Jameson started upon his conquest, he kissed her neck as this turned her on each and every time. He slowly licked and sucked on her nipples until they perked like little milk duds. He slowly entered into her womanhood and she tightly pulled him in closer and began to enjoy each stroke as he went deeper inside her.

But tonight Jameson...

Hears Don Lemon's voice on CNN

The candle was an awful smell

The bedroom had clothes thrown everywhere

The light in the half bathroom in the bedroom was still on

Tonight, was different, he was distracted by everything...

"I can't tonight Shelly, I'm sorry." Jameson gets up and begins to get dressed.

"Is it Camryn?" Shelly knows it's always Camryn. What hold does this woman have on this man?

"What the fuck, no will you stop that shit?! I have much bigger things on my mind than her ass," Jameson responds, a bit annoyed.

Shelly, whom knows this is the last night she will see him for quite some time, is irritated. "What is it then Jameson, isn't this what you want, some pussy and then you can leave anyway?" She doesn't want to pick a fight on the last night but she can't just let this go.

"Most of the time yes, but not tonight... This candle stinks, the fucking lights are on, I can hear Don Lemon's voice, this shit is distracting."

"You're such a diva," rolling her eyes and shaking her head.

"Whatever, listen. I'll be back it's not like I'm leaving forever."

"Well, why don't you talk to me? We don't have to fuck, just talk. Hold me at least, baby," Shelly pleads. She doesn't want to be alone tonight. Not this night, of all nights.

"Nope, it's too much. I just want to go home." With that Jameson finishes getting dressed, kisses Shelly and leaves.

Outside Shelly's apartment, he sits in silence in his car. "Yeah it's definitely time to go home."

2

Like Old Times

Coming back home to Pittsburgh has always been cathartic for Jameson. There is a sense of calm and relaxation he feels in his soul.

Over the past decade he has made countless trips back home during holidays, summer vacations, just to come back for the hell of it. He has never called any other city he has lived in home, because simply home is home, and nothing will or could replace that.

His foundation was set there, his bravado, his attitude, his insecurities, his imbalances all started at home. He is proud of where he is from, no place is perfect, but help mold him into the man he is today.

He made the decision to sneak into town, he already set up his lease at the Heinz Lofts, mailed boxes of clothes, had his vehicle shipped and was only waiting for his new furniture to arrive.

Home for the time being would be on the North shore, expensive ass loft apartments that sat on the Allegheny River across from downtown. Way more than he wanted to pay, but he felt it established himself as an adult back home. No need for an announcement, just show up and let everyone know at that point.

It was a cold morning, the hawk was out—as they used to say growing up—along with the salt-stained sidewalks and streets that became synonymous with winters back home.

The gray skies were also something that you grew accustomed, especially in winter. A bland, grayish-brown color of haze laid over the city for most of the winter. Every once in a while you might get a partly cloudy day to brighten your spirits, but not too often.

The ice chunks would float on the three rivers, sometime freezing over totally when the temperature really dropped. Those were the winters, like clockwork, it would be on repeat for several months until the spring would come and unthaw the city.

You could see your breath when outside, as a child, Jameson and his older brother Larry would blow their hot breath on each other while waiting for the bus—or at least until their mother would make them stop and calm down before getting on the bus.

The winters weren't so bad but he preferred the warmer winters back west, but that was about it. Nothing is like being home, nothing.

Driving through the Fort Pitt tunnels he would get the anticipation of a child opening a gift at Christmas. He already knew what it looked like, but it was simply beautiful to him. The city basically slaps you in the face with once your eyes adjust to the light during the day, however his favorite time to come home was at night.

If he was with anyone new coming home, he would always turn the music down so they could take in the view. The beautiful high rises downtown would be lit up, the rivers glistened below, depending on the time of year Heinz Field or PNC park would be lit up and illuminate the other side of the rivers as well, drive on the Fort Pitt bridge would seem as if you was stepping onto the red carpet of the city.

He always loved it...

As the car dropped him off, he checked on his loft, it was very nice but lacked any substance. He had to get some décor in this place, so it felt like home but for now he dropped off his three bags, changed into his home gear: Timbs, black Nike jogger sweats and matching top, long sleeve t-shirt, with a black skull cap... now he was truly in his element. He had to welcome himself back home...

Jameson pulls up to his old house, he pauses before he goes in. His parents live together, but have not been together for quite some time. They were older than most of his other friends parents. They tried for years to get pregnant and it happened later in life for them. He often wondered if that had something to do with their demise as they grew older.

Either way the house now was a far cry from his childhood, he recalls many great times, long road trips in the family car, birthday parties with family over, and his parents actually enjoying one another. It all came to an end once he and his brother left home, all the joy left with them.

Since then his parents have lived separate lives under the same roof. They don't hate one another, but they are no longer in love. They are ghosts walking around in a cold, dark home. No souls, just a being and having no purpose.

Inside, the house is still neatly kept. Older furniture, the plastic still is on the formal living room furniture. As a kid he hated falling asleep on them because you would almost stick to furniture when you started sweating.

The house smells like freshly cut flowers. His mother would buy a new bunch each Sunday, every Sunday of his childhood. The house is a little dusty, the stairs need to be fixed and a few cobwebs are formed in the corners of walls. After so many years of impeccable housekeeping, I guess the change fit the overall mood of the house. He goes upstairs, his mother's floor, and knocks on her door.

"Mom, it's me," Jameson says as he listens for her voice on the other side of the door.

"Boy, come in here," his mom blurts out, excited to see her boy.

His mother is sitting in a rocking chair watching the morning news on TV, KDKA or Channel 2 as she still called it, her favorite. He walks over and gives her a kiss on the forehead.

"Jameson Allen Clarkson why are you here?" she says without looking up at him.

"I missed you too... I just decided to come in early, I really didn't tell anyone I was, I just did it. I just felt like coming early. How are you?"

"I'm good, my pressure has been up some, but otherwise I'm good. Where's my grandbaby?" Eyes still locked on the TV.

"She'll be here soon, just not yet," Jameson says. He knew that question was coming sooner or later. Mother loved his daughter just as much as he did. One of the greatest joys of making her a granny.

"Well I hope you get her soon, you know her Mother ain't no good," she says matter of factly.

"She's not the best mother, but I've seen much worse." Jameson couldn't believe he just said that in support of his ex. *Interesting.*

"You going to come back to church now that you're back home?" his mother breaks his train of thought.

"I'll come visit." He expected this question, too.

Now he could feel it coming... the inevitable lecture. She talked about the same things over and over, which is why Jameson generally limited their conversations. It was either about church or his ex-wife, neither of which he felt like discussing on a consistent basis.

"Now you know you need to come back, we still got room for you."

"Mom, most of the people in that church are like 70 years old, I don't think that's a good match for me or Zanita," starting to feel annoyed, Jameson knew it was getting close to departing time.

"Well, it would be good for you and your daughter. You leave here and you don't go to church, you get this girl pregnant and now your whole life is crazy," Mom says bitterly.

"I think I'm doing pretty well, I pray, I treat people right, I just don't want to go to church every Sunday, and Tuesday and Wednesday and Friday..."

"Oh boy, stop it!"

"Seriously you go every day almost," Jameson says.

"Better than most places."

"I guess so..." He stands up. "Where is Dad?"

"Oh he's downstairs I'm sure. That's where he always is," Mom says, eyes still locked on the TV.

"Good to see you, Mom, I have some running around to do. I'll see you soon." Jameson hugs his mother and walks downstairs.

In the living room there are still pictures of the family, his parents and his brother. They used to run around and make all kinds of noise in this room. Their father would listen to old jazz records... Miles, Coltrane, just to name a few.

His favorite times were around the holidays when the entire house would be filled with his aunts, uncles, cousins and family friends. It was a house full of character, love and warmth. Now he looked around and it was gray, cold and desolate. Dust laid around picture frames, books that sat in the same place for years.

In the basement, his father was sleep. His man cave was a collection of artifacts. Old jazz albums stacked in milk carts take up almost an entire corner; as a kid he and his brother would fumble through them while his parents were gone.

The collection was impressive, he loved the way vinyl records would sound when they played. His love and appreciation of various forms of music spawned from his father.

Dad has a huge flat screen television that Jameson bought for him a couple years ago. It's on sports, that's all he watches now. His cigar is still lit, and in the ash tray. His father has his house slippers on, matching pajamas and his Kangol. He was always the original GQ dresser in the family.

"Dad, wake up." Jameson nudges his father on the arm.

His Father grabs his glasses.

"Hey boy, what the hell you doing here?" A little discombobulated and not really sure if he's dreaming or this is his Jameson standing there in front of him. Closing and re-opening his eyes, he reaches out for his son.

They give each other a hug and sit down.

"I came in early, I wanted to see everyone before I got started at the station," Jameson says, looking around the man cave.

"Always great to see you. How's my granddaughter?" Zanita is the apple of her granddad's eye.

"She's not happy I'm gone but she's doing well. I just need to get myself together before I bring her out here."

"Yeah, good idea. Maybe you'll find a good woman to help you too," his father says, looking side eye over at his son.

They both laugh.

"I don't know about that but I know I'll be able to take care of her on my own if needed."

"Yeah, of course you can. How is the new station?"

"I don't know yet, obviously we've done interviews, Zoom calls, phone calls, emails, but being in person, every day could be different. I'm excited and nervous," Jameson says. He always had that bond with his father that he could admit his insecurities and vulnerabilities, and still remain a 'man'.

"I remember when you was 9 or 10 years old, you used to get so anxious about anything new. School, meeting new people, playing on a new team... You know who always calmed you down? ...Larry," his father pointed out.

"Absolutely, he was my idol growing up."

"Yes, he was."

"How you been feeling?" Jameson's attempt to change the subject.

"I'm good, don't worry about your dad, I am always good. I keep being blessed with a new day. I enjoy each day. Now your mother, that's a different story."

They both laugh again.

"She means well, she's just herself," Jameson says.

"Yeah, herself is too much."

"Yeah she can be for sure. Dad, I gotta get out of here, you need anything?" Jameson sits up on the edge of the couch.

"Only one thing, now that you are home. Don't be a stranger son," his father says and smiles.

"I promise." Jameson gets up, hugs his father and leaves.

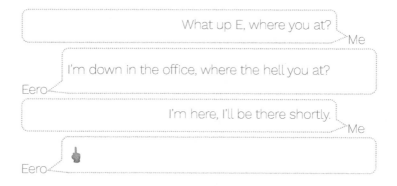

Jameson drives through his old neighborhood, the historic Hill District. Many stories, many days and nights running through these streets, and it all helped him become the man he is today. As a kid growing up there was projects, a lot of drugs, gangs... now there are empty lots, closed businesses and the start of gentrification is trickling in.

They even renamed part of the neighborhood above downtown when they put up some new houses, the trickery never ends. It saddens him that so many small, black-owned businesses are gone. The corner of Centre and Kirkpatrick used to buzz with barbershops, corner stores, a gas station, mom and pop shops... now it was deserted. Old signs and broken windows took the place of kids running up and down the streets and black entrepreneurship.

Despite the desolateness of his old neighborhood, he still felt proud. There was a great history in these old streets and buildings. He hopes to be part of the resurgence of his old neighborhood.

He arrives at Eero's downtown office and takes a seat in the waiting area. Jameson looks around the office, pictures of Eero with various dignitaries are scattered throughout. Various other awards and certificates are placed neatly on end tables or on the walls. Jameson has always thought of Eero as an amazing man, father, and friend. The respect they have for one another is mutual and admirable.

Eero Williams emerges from his office, the city of Pittsburgh's first black elected City Controller, stood around 5'11 inches—although he always said he was 6 feet—light complexion, as always in impeccable shape, he runs a couple miles a day, weighs about 190 pounds of pure muscle.

Self-confident, calm, collected, and always dressed as if he is going on a GQ cover shoot. He has locks down past his shoulders, wears designer suits to work every day, and hard framed glasses.

Eero was always amazing with numbers, Jameson would always cheat off his math tests in school, he never really left Pittsburgh, he married his high school sweetheart, went to Pitt

University, he went on to get his MBA, and was a co-founder of a start-up financial firm, sold it before turning 30, he eventually wanted to give back and decided he would run for elected office. He won in a landslide and has held the position since.

However, this upcoming year he will have some stiff competition for his seat, and the stress is starting to show.

Eero walks over to Jameson and they both embrace.

"It's been a minute bruh, good to see you," Eero says to Jameson.

"Too long but I'm here."

They both walk into his office. The office is very simple. A desk, with two seats in front of it, a round table towards the back, a few book shelves, his wedding picture hangs on the wall, and on his desk is a picture of his wife and another of his two children.

"Why you always sneaking into town? You could let me know, I'll come get you, I tell you that all the time."

"Nah, I like to pop up on y'all. Anyway, how you living, you look a little disheveled?" Jameson quickly switches the subject.

"Here you go with those SAT prep words and shit. Do I look that bad?" Eero asked jokingly.

"I know you, your tie is undone, your glasses aren't on, call it a lucky guess if you want," Jameson says.

Eero shrugs.

"There's a few things going on... the election, wife, grown people shit I guess."

"Being grown is definitely some bullshit at times I agree. How are the babies doing?"

"They're always good, just getting old and spending more money every day," Eero says with the biggest smile on his face. "When are you bringing Z out?"

"Hopefully once I get settled, the new show will be 7 – 10 pm. It couldn't be at a worse time to be a single dad, so I don't know what the hell I'm gonna do, but I'll figure it out. Maybe get a nanny or something..." Jameson shrugs his shoulders.

"That's that big money right there, getting nanny's, loft apartments, luxury vehicles... I need to be more like you Dr. Black Love," Eero teases.

"Fuck outta here, I've been blessed for sure. But you got all this (points to his wife and kids), that's more valuable than money."

"Sometimes I wonder, especially with her," he looks over at the picture of his wife and sighs.

"Well, you knew how she was from high school, that was all you playa. You just had the have the prettiest red-bone in school," Jameson recollects.

"Just following your lead, Jameson, just trying to be like you," Eero teases and laughs.

"You can't ever be like me, you're way better than I am."

"Yeah you right, I am," Eero agrees. His phone rings and Eero picks it up.

"No, I'll be there. No problem."

Eero hangs up the phone.

"I gotta have a meeting with my staff shortly."

"No problem, I'm gonna run by the bar and check on Kolby," Jameson says and stands up to leave.

"I'll get with you this evening, great to have you home," Eero says and he reaches for Jameson.

They give each other dap and Jameson leaves.

Kolby Richardson stands at 6'5, keeps a freshly cut low fade, his beard is neatly trimmed, skin color is milk chocolate, tipping the scales at 225 pounds. His typical daily attire is sweats, Jordan's, a thick chain around his neck and one of his multitude of wrist watches on his wrist.

He has never lacked for confidence, at least outwardly, is the first to speak and also makes sure he gets the last word in as well, and loves to gamble.

Since a young child, he has always been about his money. He would sell white kids penny candy for 10 cents in school because they didn't have corner stores. His entrepreneurial spirit led him to using his money from his mother to buy a cheap duplex. With that money and his loan money from college, he purchased another duplex, a small 4-unit apartment complex.

After that, he dropped out of school and has never looked back. Now he owns multiple houses, a few smaller apartment complexes, a lounge and a trucking company.

His favorite place to be is his bar named after its owner of course... he drinks for free and he can be as loud as he wants, perfect for Kolby.

Jameson walks in and sees Kolby talking to a group of younger men.

"That's why we need to put our money together," Kolby says, "If I come in with money and you come in with money, then can't nobody stop us. Shit, why you think I still keep this bar open?"

Jameson walks over and interrupts them.

"So your punk ass can drink for free..." Jameson slyly says.

Kolby looks up quickly but then realizes it's Jameson.

"Man, what the fuck..."

They give each other dap and a hug.

"Pete, you gotta give me a minute. This is my brother here."

Pete nods at both gentlemen and walks away.

"What you drinking J?" Kolby turns to Jameson.

"Give me a Tito's and Sprite, just keep it easy."

"Fuck that, we doing a shot. Your ass is about to blow up, you back home. We not doing no punk ass drinks right now. You been out in that sun too long," Kolby says.

Kolby goes behind the bar and pours two double shots of Hennessy.

"Come on with the henny, Bruh."

"This is it, put hair on your chest," Kolby says as he hands one of the shot glasses to Jameson.

"I don't know why black people drink this shit..." Jameson says frowning at the glass in front of him.

"They made this for us Jameson, this is the black man's love potion, you know how many babies have been made from Hennessy?"

Kolby lifts up his shot glass and Jameson reluctantly joins him.

"To my man, my dawg, my ace Jameson Clarkson, aka Dr. Black Love, aka I will steal yo bitch if you slippin, aka my brother. Love you."

"Love you too, K," Jameson says.

They both take the shots, Jameson coughs a little. Kolby pours another and drinks it straight.

"Slow down there K."

"I'm good. So let's talk. Come upstairs."

They walk upstairs into Kolby's office.

The office is a little small but so is the building. Kolby lights a cigar and takes a seat behind his desk.

"I appreciate you arranging for the loft, it's beautiful."

"That was nothing, I used to date one of the chicks in the office, it was an easy phone call," explains Kolby, Jameson laughs.

"Of course you did... How is business?"

"Here its always so-so, same people drink basically. I need to probably sell this place but I can't. I'd feel guilty if I did. It don't make a ton of money, but people that come here love it. It's a Pittsburgh staple at this point," Kolby boasts proudly and sadly at the same time.

"Yeah I hear you and it just so happens to be named Kolby's so you can see your damn name every day," Jameson jokes and they both laugh to lighten the mood again.

"That helps for sure. So, what's your plan?" Kolby asks.

"I'll be here for a bit before the show starts, just trying to get settled in. I need to have everything in order before we kick things off. Then I'll figure out how I'll bring Z back out here."

"You always want life to be a straight line, been trying to tell you to ride them curves all our lives."

"Your ass rides too many curves," Jameson laughs.

"Here you go, these women are just something to do most of the time. I'm focused on my money as always."

"I will say amen to that. You have literally always been focused on money," Jameson says.

"You the baller now, you got a big time contract, we waiting for that book deal or something next," Kolby teases.

"One thing at a time, I need to focus and make sure this new show pops off."

Jameson looks at the clock on the wall.

"I need to get back and lay it down, meeting with the new team tomorrow morning." Jameson gets up and he and Kolby embrace.

Jameson says his good-byes and drives back to his new home.

3

Game Plan

*J*ameson wakes up feeling ambivalent. On one hand he was feeling the anticipation as if it was the first day of kindergarten.

He was going to his new place of work, where he worked so many years to develop and grow his Dr. Black Love persona. All those long nights writing, posting, responding to complete strangers but helping people had led him to this point.

On the other hand he felt anxious, and mainly as a shortcoming of his he had learned over the years. He was not one for making friends easily, and even less so about opening up and being friendly—or fake as he liked to call it.

He hated small talk, the bullshit conversation about someone's past that always come up at dinner parties, corporate events and the like. He would much rather not talk than have those conversations. And with an entirely new staff, he knew that would come with it.

With that on his mind he took the short drive over the 16th Street Bridge to downtown and parked. Gave himself a quick pep talk and walked into the new station, home.

After being seated for a few moments, he heard the voice of Justin Strong, the Station Manager, he was always loud and causing ruckus. He was appointed to this position as his family was very powerful in the industry and he was assigned this station to show his leadership skills and move to an even bigger market. All he cared about was ratings—the better the ratings, the quicker he could leave the city.

Abraham Bernstein, the Program Director for his show was with Justin. Throughout the interview and offer stages Jameson and Abraham grew to have a mutual respect for one another. Jameson felt their visions aligned with where the show could and would go in the future. And in his role that was vitally important, back west Jameson was basically his own Program Director, that would not be the case at his new home.

They both greeted Jameson.

"My man Jameson Clarkson," exclaimed Justin.

"Good to see you again Justin. I'm excited to get things started."

They shake hands.

"Jameson, glad your back home and with us sir," says Abraham.

They shake hands.

"Let's get back and get started on things, we have some further development that we feel will help the show Jameson," says Justin.

Jameson thinks to himself, *here goes the bullshit.*

They all walk back to a conference room and sit down.

Justin claps his hands and begins to talk...

"Jameson, we're glad to have you here. Throughout the process, I hope you could sincerely feel our want to bring you here and turn your show into a national brand. During our recruitment of you, we laid some ground work for where we thought things would go. But, we feel there needs to be a couple of changes to the show itself."

Jameson interrupts, "So this is where you try to stick me once I sign on the dotted line?"

"Not even close Jameson, let me further explain," responds Justin as he sits up nervously in his chair and clears his throat.

"We can dig through the research and numbers later, but the biggest change, or better yet addition, to your show is going to be a co-host."

Justin pauses to get a read on Jameson.

Jameson slowly nods as if telling Justin to continue telepathically.

"How do you feel about that?" asks Justin.

"How do you feel about it, Justin? It really doesn't matter what I feel, right?" Jameson says. *Breathe Jameson, breathe...*

Abraham, sensing the growing tension, interjects.

"Jameson, let me give some context as to why we feel this would be a valuable move and asset to the Dr. Black Love show," Abraham continues, "There is an additional element that can be of value, the ability to bounce ideas, concepts, conversation between yourself and your co-host. Ultimately they will allow you to focus on what you do best... give amazing advice, be honest and help people. Ultimately, if it doesn't work, we'll take a look at things but..."

Justin interrupts, "This will work, Jameson, trust us."

There is a brief period of silence for five seconds, but feels more like 30 for Jameson. He has never worked with anyone on his show, he always felt like he could do it on his own. The work he put into his moniker and character meant a lot to him. He developed it on his own, with little help from anyone and even less belief in what he was doing. He would see and hear the doubt in the few individuals that he told about his idea.

Nobody will listen to a black male about love, you all are the worst at it.

He was literally told by a former friend of his whom he often bounced ideas off. So, he said to hell with anyone and did it on his own. Day by day, response by response, one like lead to two, and so forth.

"Here's the thing, this is more than a character for me. Dr. Black Love is me, he's a part of me. And not that someone else can't help, but I don't know... Who the hell is it?" Jameson asks.

"Great question," exclaimed Justin.

Justin picks up the phone in the middle of the table and says, "Send in Keisha."

Jameson is a little perplexed.

Keisha Washington is a beautiful young woman. She stood about 5'7 inches, smooth milk chocolate skin, hair that fell to her shoulders, beautiful teeth, and a body to kill for.

Jameson thinks to himself, *"Damn, she too fine to work with."*

Jameson stands up and introduces himself.

"Hello Keisha, my name is Jameson..."

She cuts him off, "Clarkson, yes I am very aware of who you are, Mr. Clarkson."

"No need to be so formal, just call me Jameson."

"I will actually call you Dr. Black Love most of the time," Keisha says flirting a little. She just landed a once-in-a-lifetime gig to sit next to Dr. Black Love himself, every single day. *Keep your cool, girl.*

Jameson laughs at the flirtatious comment and takes a seat. Keisha sits next to him.

"What do you think Jameson?" asks Justin.

"I mean… I don't know Keisha has a lot going for her. No, I don't know her but I think she's worth taking a look at. I don't mean that, I mean she's worth seeing if it will work," Jameson fumbles all over himself. Feeling embarrassed, he looks at Justin and Abraham for a life guard.

Abraham sensing that Jameson is a bit thrown off by Keisha steps in and slides Keisha's resume over to him.

"Keisha brings a lot to the table, she's hosted several shows in the DMV area, she graduated from the Newhouse School of Public Communications at Syracuse, she's hosted several podcasts, she'll be a lovely addition to the show we feel."

"What do you know about the show Miss, or is it Mrs., Washington?" asks Jameson.

"Ms. Washington for now at least, Jameson. I know that you built the show on your own, which I respect a lot. It's not easy for a man in the industry that you have built your career in. You are very honest which I really appreciate in a man, and your audience loves that about you… But…"

"But what?" asks Jameson.

Keisha continues, "I feel like you could give more of yourself to your audience. Your audience has a feel for what you think, but not who Jameson Clarkson is behind the advice you give. I believe *that* is where I can be the most valuable as your co-host."

Jameson sits back and takes in what Keisha just mentioned.

"That's why we..." Justin starts to speak.

"Hold on Justin, so you're saying that I'm not personal enough with my audience, interesting," Jameson staring at Keisha. She got balls.

"What I mean is I feel that adding a female perspective and digging deeper with you will propel the show to a new stratosphere, Jameson. Ultimately allowing you to have a cult like following, because they will relate to you even better."

"I like that idea, let's make it work," says Jameson to everyone.

"Perfect, we'll get started on some ideas over the next week or so," says Abraham.

Everyone stands up and shakes hands.

As they all exit the room, Jameson taps Keisha on the shoulder, "Can we grab some coffee or something downstairs?"

"They have coffee up here, Jameson."

"They do… well I'd like to take you to get some coffee downstairs, so we can talk outside of these walls if that makes sense. Like, we should get to know each other before we step up to the mic and present ourselves as co-hosts."

Keisha smiles and nods her head in agreement.

Downstairs at the coffee shop the conversation continues…

"So Keisha, where are you from?" Jameson asks.

"Right outside of D.C., went to Syracuse and bounced around a few markets. The typical young person's path in radio or television, hoping to land on a show that won't get canceled in two weeks. And trust me, that's happened to me before. So now I am here."

"They brought you in for the show specifically?"

"Not exactly, but once I found out you agreed to come, I pitched the idea to Abraham and it took off from there. I follow you on the 'Gram, and grew to appreciate what you do. So I literally just told him what I thought you needed for radio and he agreed."

"I thought about having a co-host before, but just didn't do it," Jameson admits.

"Why is that?"

"It just takes a lot for me to put what I've worked for in someone else's hands."

"So you don't trust anyone?"

"I do trust a few people but not many. Everyone has their own agendas and that probably will not line up with mine and my vision for the show. So, why bother?"

"For me, I'm the co-host, this is your show. I just want to help you steer the train the right way so we get enough riders, or listeners in this case, to make it a hit. That being said, I look forward to working with you, Mr. Clarkson."

"Girl you better stop that shit."

They both laugh.

"Well Jameson, I need to get upstairs and get back to work. I don't get all the perks you get as the hot shot host. And I think you have a young lady gawking at you anyway over there. Maybe she's another fan of yours..." Keisha points her head towards an admiring fan across the room.

Jameson turns and pierces the room looking for the accused woman. He then catches her eyes.

Keisha taps him on his chest slightly, "Have a great day Dr. Black Love," and walks away.

"OK, Keisha, I will see you soon."

Ryann Davis stares back in disbelief.

They meet one another half way and give a long, deliberate hug.

Jameson thinks to himself, *"Damn she always smelled so good. Literally everything about her always did."*

"Ryann Davis, how are you?" Jameson asks while gazing into her eyes.

"I am doing well, surprised to see you here."

"Have a seat, please." Jameson points to a nearby seat at the coffee shop.

"No, I have to go back into the office."

"Where do you work?"

"Across the street, I run a non-profit, not that you pay attention to anything going on with me," Ryan blurts out. She hasn't seen or heard from Jameson in a minute, now he's in town again.

"I do but how about we go to dinner and catch up. I'll come pick you up tonight?" Jameson hopes for the best. Ryann is the one that got away, maybe this is fate happening all over again. But baby steps, dinner first.

"No, you are not picking me up," Ryan interrupts his thoughts, "I know you too well. I will drive myself to meet you Jameson."

Ryann begins to walk away.

"I don't have your number," Jameson calls out.

Ryann stops and turns, "Check your pocket," and again walks away.

Jameson checks his front pocket and Ryann's business card is in there. He smiles and immediately sends her a text message.

I will pick you up at 7 pm.
Me

Ryann stops and looks at her phone, without turning, smiles and responds.

Ryann
No, I will meet your ass at 7 pm. Not falling for that anymore, I'm grown.

Fine, I'll figure out where to go.
Me

4

Ex to the Next

Jameson and Ryann are led to their seats by the waiter. Jameson pulls the chair out for Ryann, she sits and he follows.

Jameson takes a look at Ryann, she looks the same. Ryann, neatly combed hair, mocha colored skin, flawless pearly white teeth, slight scar under her right eye—which in Jameson's eyes is the only flaw on her entire body—sugary lips with a hint of lip gloss.

She is wearing an off white dress that shows enough cleavage to gain your interest, but not stare too long, nails neatly done, a couple bracelets, simple yet beautiful as always.

"Are you just going to stare at me or are we going to talk, Mr. Clarkson?" Ryann says as she tries to keep her composure. *Damn this dude is fine!*

"I'm sorry, just admiring you," Jameson wastes no time with flirting.

"Here you go, always the charmer. Is your wife out here with you?" Ryann asks intriguingly. She always had a certain sassiness that attracted and repelled Jameson at the same time.

He slowly shakes his head and smiles at the reminder.

"Ryann you know I'm not married anymore, just like everyone else. I know if nobody else told you, Kolby's loud ass did."

"Yes, he did of course, he always calls me about you," Ryann says giggling.

"Kolby always thought you was the one."

"That's because I should have been and you know it."

"We was young, too young to be worried about forever."

"If that's the case, then why are we here, Jameson?"

"Because we aren't young anymore, and I'm back," he says matter of factly; then the waiter walks over to the table and interrupts the flow but Jameson nods him off.

"So, tell me about your non-profit, what do you do, how long you been running it..." Jameson continues.

"If I know you, you already know the answers to all those questions."

"Actually I didn't but I did plan to, you know me."

"Yes, I do. It's fairly new, and if you had actually kept in touch with me, you would know that I'm very passionate about giving opportunities to young brown girls. So our non-profit helps develop talent, as well as find internships for high school and college young ladies around the country. We mainly focus on engineering and technology, but other areas as well."

"That's very impressive. But I expect nothing less from you."

"I appreciate that, I love what I do, finally."

"Me too," Jameson agrees.

"Yes, Dr. Black Love. Sometimes I don't know if it's you or someone else on the radio giving advice."

"Why the hell would you say that?"

"Just seems too perfect, like you are honestly amazing at being introspective, honest and open. Yet, in real life, you are nothing like that," Ryann boasts.

"I think I have grown up some, I just try to go off what I learned to this point in my own life and others. I feel like I have been through enough to give some wisdom about something most of us fail miserably at, and that's love," he feels like he's stating his case. And failing miserably.

"So you don't see the irony in that speaking to me?" Ryann getting to her hidden agenda.

Jameson pauses before responding. They have history, and some of it is not pretty, but he knew the conversation would lead to this so he was prepared.

"Ryann, look I know I basically just left. I didn't know what to do, you really didn't give me any options."

"Do you think you deserved options?" Ryann's voice starts to escalate slightly.

"At that time, no I do not. But what else was I supposed to do? You told me you would never forgive me, you told me you would never give me another chance. For a young man like myself at 24 years old, I took you for your word, and I left," an explanation long overdue.

"And ran all the way to the other side of the country, get some chick pregnant, have a baby with *her* and basically act like I never existed?" Now she's pissed.

"That's not fair, and not totally accurate."

"Do you not have a baby momma now?"

"I hate that phrase, it's so damn disrespectful."

Ryann rolls her eyes and begins to read the menu.

Jameson continues.

"All I am saying is that she's my ex-wife and the mother to my daughter, so at least show some respect for that. I don't love her and she damn sure isn't my best friend, but I have to respect that much at least," Jameson says in a serious tone.

"Fine."

"So, where is your boyfriend?" Trying to lighten the mood, things are starting to heat up way too soon.

"I don't have one, nor do I want one," she replies.

"I know you've dated since us, you aren't a nun now," Jameson pries.

"No, I'm not but I'm not a hoe either. So I keep to myself, I may go out here and there, but I don't even have any possibles at this point," Ryan says as she searches Jameson's face for a reaction.

"You and me both."

"Really... who was you with this afternoon. She looks like more than a possible, she's pretty, you should date her." *The games we play.*

"I just met her, and she is going to be my co-host." *So she does care. I knew it.*

She puts down her menu and shakes her head.

"Lord, please help that girl."

Jameson shakes his head at her response.

"Within two weeks, you'll have her over to your place and that'll be it. I know how you are, I hate that about you. Women just throw themselves at you, all the time. Ever since high school, I can't stand it."

"I don't know about all that, but if nothing else I am always professional. That's how I feed myself and my daughter, so no one night stand or any relationship with someone I work for is worth that."

"That's a great response but it's a damn lie."

They both laugh at each other.

"After dinner, I want us to go somewhere."

"I told you, you are not driving me and we are damn sure not going back to your place, Jameson."

"Neither of those, I promise. Just follow me in your own car then."

After dinner, Jameson leads Ryann while they drive separately through downtown, to the South side. Throughout the ride they small talk on the speaker phone, smile and look at the city. They get on the incline and get off at Mt. Washington. They get out, walk to one of the benches and take a seat.

"I have not been up here in a long time," says Jameson.

"You do realize that we came up here for our first official date?" Ryann asks.

"Of course, that's why we came back here."

"I feel like you're up to something," she looks at Jameson for clues.

"No, I honestly love the view and I knew we used to come up so I just wanted to share the moment with you... Look Ryann, regardless of what I say to you, I can never take the hurt away that I caused you. Believe it or not, I was hurt too."

"Yet you ran away," she blurted out. She can't help it. She's mad still, after all of these years. But she can't help but feel something more. Something unavoidable.

"I'm back now at least," Jameson interrupts her thoughts.

"Negro, please. You came back here for a job, not for me. And we luckily saw one another while you was trying to pimp some other chick."

"Nothing happens without a reason."

"Maybe it was just to have a nice dinner, you to say sorry and that's it."

"Perhaps or maybe not."

"What do you want, Jameson?"

"All I want is for you to say yes to date number two."

"Maybe. But for now, I need to go home."

Jameson nods in agreement, helps Ryann to her feet, and they walk towards the incline.

5

Eero's Castle

*E*ero is sitting at home in his office. His two children, son Emmanuel, 6, and daughter Deborah, 4, are playing in front of his desk, making a little too much noise, but he is attempting to deal with it as he often feels he doesn't get to spend as much time as he would like with them.

There are papers all over his desk, he has a lot of proposals to review and his own re-election to prepare for. In his mind, he has much to do and little time to get it done.

Off in the distance, his wife, Mary Williams, sits on the couch watching television. Mary is a stay-at-home mom, by her choice. She comes from money, and despite Eero's continuous concerns about money, they are well off.

Eero sold a company at a young age as a partner, his wife's family will never let them go without, and he makes good money in his position for the City.

Eero leans back and sighs to himself.

"Daddy, why are you tired?" asks Emmanuel. As he comes over and sits on his father's lap, Eero gave his son a hug.

As Eero became a father, there were several things he wanted to do differently than his father had done with him. One of the biggest holes Eero felt he had to overcome as an adult was the lack of emotion and compassion he would feel in moments when he knew he should have some, he had nothing to give.

As he continued in his relationship with his wife, he eventually came to believe that he was never shown that type of love by either of his parents growing up. As he began to speak more freely and openly about it with his friends, he realized that for many black people, showing emotion, especially as a black man equated to being soft or weak.

Therefore, generation to generation passed the torch of showing more tough love, although a form of love but not truly expressing the wider ranges of love, and ultimately that impacted relationships—friendships or romantic ones.

Once he figured this out, he was determined to break that mold of being cold to your offspring. Eero worked diligently at showing his daughter and son, all sides of him as a man. And he made sure to tell his son that he loved him, that he cared for him, that men do cry, that men are allowed to have feelings of doubt at times, that men are human beings.

Every night he kissed both of his children and told them he loved them, every morning before they went to school, he did the same.

He also held his son since the first day he was born. Mothers have an internal connection that fathers will never have, but Eero developed his own. He held his young son to show him love, compassion, and for him to never think less of himself as a man that showed emotions.

"Son, that's because Daddy works really hard."

"You should take a break and come play with me. When I get tired, playing makes me happy."

"That's a great idea, Emmanuel. What are you playing?"

They crawl onto the floor and begin playing.

After a few moments, Eero crawls over to Deborah who is listening to her iPad with her headphones on.

Eero pulls one of her headphones away from ear and blows hard.

"Daddy!" screams Deborah.

He begins to tickle them both, and they grow increasingly louder as he continues to tickle torture them both.

Mary slowly walks into the room.

"It's time for bed for all little children."

"Mom, come on. Daddy never goes to bed early," says Emmanuel.

"I'll come up to see you. Listen to your mother," Eero says. He gives both of them a kiss and they walk past Mary to go upstairs.

"We need to talk when I come back down," Mary says to Eero. An eerie feeling runs down his spine as he watches her follow the kids out of the office.

That was the last thing Eero needed to hear tonight.

After about 10-15 minutes, Eero continues to twist his hair, something he did when he was anxious, Mary finally walks into the office.

"Are you working?" asks Mary.

"No, no man works when his wife says we need to talk. That's the worst thing you can say to me while I'm actually trying to work."

"What do we need to do to win the campaign?"

"That's what you want to talk about right now? Same thing we always do, get word out early, be present in the community and make sure we represent a strong, united family."

"Yeah about that last point," Mary states.

Here we go. Eero asks, "What about it Mary?"

"I'm not really feeling the strong, united family lane is gonna work. Your main competition is not married, he's white and has no children. In your position, that seems like someone that has more time to dedicate to working for the city," she points out.

"What makes you so concerned... You've never asked me anything outside of what do we need to wear, what time do we need to arrive, shit like that. Now you're trying to tell me how to run my campaign?"

"I never thought you could lose before. And I am not married to a loser, just remember that."

"What is that supposed to mean?"

"It means do not lose, Eero, do whatever we need to do to win. So prepare now, see how things are going, and then we'll figure it out."

"Who is we?"

"Whoever we needs to be."

"Now you sound like your Dad."

"Nothing is wrong with that, he's not a loser either." Mary gets up and walks out of the room without saying another word.

Eero has always appreciated Mary's family, he has learned a great deal from her father, Mr. Nicholson. He was his first investor when his investment firm was started and he has always given him great advice.

But there are times when he has wanted some distance between them, so he and his wife could flourish and not be under their shadow. Eero's dedication to wanting to improve the city itself led him to take the position several years ago. He wasn't going to be controlled, or use questionable tactics to win, he had no need to do that.

Eero walks into the other room and stands in front of her view.

"Can you move please, I get like an hour to watch TV each night and it's my time," Mary says, looking around Eero.

"Listen, I appreciate your father's offer, but we don't need to do anything that could come back to bite us later. And quite frankly I'm disappointed that you don't believe in me more than that."

"Eero quit being sensitive. You're running for public office, having people in the right places always helps."

Eero gets on his knees and is eye to eye with Mary.

"We'll win, I promise." Eero gives Mary a kiss on the lips. He continues by kissing on her neck and begins to slip her nightgown off, but she pulls away.

"Eero, I'm tired. I just don't feel like it tonight."

Mary stands up and turns off the TV.

"That's always your excuse."

"No, it's reality. I take care of your kids all day, and that's the main reason your ass better not lose." Mary walks away quickly.

Eero turns around and sits on the floor.

The house is quiet and cold now. He stares around and looks at his home. He has beautiful furniture, a nice house, beautiful children and a beautiful wife.

He thinks to himself, *"All these material items and I still have nothing to show for it. We're just dying painfully and slowly."*

6

Dear Dr. Black Love (Part 1)

ameson's character of Dr. Black Love grew organically online one email response at a time. As his base grew, he eventually started posting video responses on Instagram and Facebook; and as he grew in popularity, this all led to the start of his show.

At the essence of what he has always believed kept the show real and authentic is him being responsive and real to his listeners. He has always struck a chord with women, but eventually men started to slowly buy in as well.

He would even have individuals brave enough to be live on the air with him, sometimes without showing their faces.

Throughout the transition moving back home and starting a re-branded show, he has continued to give back to people in need as he always has done.

Letter with his response on Instagram live...

Jameson is opening his live stream...

"Dr. Black Love is here again people. I apologize but moving across the country is not an easy process. So we are a bit backed up, but we will be doing these routinely moving forward. And don't forget the new show will be coming to you soon, with some exciting additions and upgrades to the show overall. So let's get started with a letter from a young lady."

Jameson reads...

"Dear Dr. Black Love, I love the show and my girlfriends and I end up having debates about what you say or what we'd say. And then it dawned on me that I needed your help. I will try to keep this short... I have two amazing men and I feel that I am in love with them both. Yeah I know, most people say it's impossible, but I think if I'm not in love, I like them both A LOT.

I travel so I will admit it allows me to enjoy them both and not have to worry about anything. Neither of them are needy, they both are strong black men, have amazing careers and are awesome. For me, I know part of it just not wanting to commit to anything outside of the time we spend together.

The reason I am writing is I am concerned that I may lose them both, and I don't want to after two years of dating. At some point with any relationship and being stereotypical the woman will catch emotions despite knowing what she was getting into and it changes things. In my situation, one of the two is making strong hints he wants more. The other is content on staying with what we have. Therein lies the problem, any decision may require me to lose one of them.

So, my question is should I just tell the other one to kick rocks, tell them both or just be alone? All three thoughts have ran through my mind, been chewed on, spit out and regurgitated again and again. Help me Dr. Black Love.

Signed,

Two Timing Sista and Loving It"

Jameson addresses the audience...

"First of all, I love the name Two Timing Sista and Loving It. That is quite creative and self-reflecting of who you are and owning it. We talk about that all the time. I would love to get her live so we could really dig in, perhaps we can do that when the new show kicks off here shortly. We'll work on that for you all. For now we will go with what we have.

Over the years we have a few principles that we feel that all relationships should have. And one of the main ones we have agreed to and accepted is that honesty is a cornerstone of any relationship. Doesn't matter the type of relationship, it just needs to be there, period.

Having said that, it doesn't appear that Two Timing Sista is being totally honest. And maybe to give her the benefit of the doubt, she doesn't have to be. Perhaps the men are good with seeing her when they do and that's it; some men, if they getting some, they don't really care about much else. If that's the case then so be it, everyone is happy and to each his own.

I'm going to read in-between the lines and guess Two Timing has some type of career where she can travel, so she's able to bounce around and not be under suspicion from either man. So they see her when she can, and outside of that they just play it cool.

But now we get faced with a new reality, which typically happens, someone wants something more, or they want more than they're getting. Having 50% of someone is cool for a while but normally we want it all, as humans we're greedy.

Here's what I think you should do, and again this is just my opinion. I'll go in reverse order of your questions... Should you just be alone? Perhaps that is your least favorite answer. Few of us want to be alone, if any. I would say 'yes' if you are tired of the back and forth, having to keep track of things, perhaps if you have to lie about things to keep them the way they have been. If not, and you have no trepidation about two timing then so be it.

Truthfully, there are definitely individuals that can roll that way, and many of us do it for some time, but you have been doing this for a couple of years. My question is why? Are you afraid of commitment, have you been hurt and in order to prevent being hurt you keep a harem to make yourself feel better even perhaps? Only you can answer those questions.

Should you tell them both? This one is trickier, I feel that the one dude that is asking you for more, you should definitely tell. That can be very difficult to do, it's hard letting your guard down and exposing your dirty laundry, so to speak. And I know that is somewhat difficult for you, otherwise you would have just done it when he asked initially and let the cards fall where they may.

And the reason I say you have to tell him is because, honestly he asked. If he never asked and there is no real covenant of sorts made then so be it. But I feel if he is asking and put in time with you, he deserves to know.

Now, should you tell the other? Yes, but not yet. I feel they both deserve to know. Obviously once the first one knows that may determine when you tell the other ...but let's just say Male A says, *I'm good with that*. Then you need to tell Male B immediately because, at that point, I feel like you would be lying to him if you did not. If Male A says *he can't do it,* then you'll only have Male B. Then you make that determination so, at some point they both need to know, it's just a matter of when.

The first question I think is irrelevant and I do not believe you would want to just tell the other one to kick rocks. If that was the case, you would not have even bothered to send your story in. Give them both the respect you would want if the shoe was on the other foot.

Please, Miss Two Timing, give us a follow-up, I would love to have you live on the show for that one.

Thank you all, and remember... love only enters if the heart is willing, signing off Dr. Black Love."

Jameson takes the headphones off, shuts off the mic, and sits back to bask in the after show moment.

7

Call From Ryann

F ameson is driving in the evening when he receives an incoming call from Ryann. He lets it ring and go to voice mail, he waits a couple minutes and calls back. Just something that he does—don't appear too desperate, or too needy.

"Hey Ryann, I apologize I was on a call," he lies.

"I know you're always so busy Mr. Clarkson. I apologize for disturbing you," Ryann says sarcastically.

"No need to apologize. What's going on?"

"I am such a great person as you well know, I felt obligated to do something I know you'd appreciate. You remember Adam from high school?"

"Yeah I do, Adam Franklin. He played in the band, dude ended up having a group or something didn't he?"

"That's him, well he obviously didn't make it as a singer, but he ended up going to journalism for school and does some work for various outlets, including the Pittsburgh Courier."

"That's dope, how do you keep in touch with all these people?" Jameson is intrigued and turned on at the same time.

"Listen, in the non-profit world, you need friends in all places. But anyway, I reached out to him and he wants to do a piece on you for the paper, well it's online now like most..."

"Word, that's wassup," Jameson interrupts, "The Courier is legendary, I'd love to do it."

"Good because he needs you to do it tomorrow to make the next issue," Ryann says dryly.

"I don't have nothing but time right now, speaking of which when are we going out again?" Jameson shoots his shot.

"This is a professional call, Mr. Clarkson, I need you to stay focused," she smiles at the slight flirtation.

"I can multi-task, as you well know."

"Multi-task and keep your eyes on the damn road, Jameson. I'll text you his info but get in touch with him ASAP."

"I will do that, and I appreciate it Ryann."

"I know you do... I need to go but let me know how it goes."

"Of course I will, when can I take you out again?" Jameson shoots his shot again. No harm in going in for another chance.

"Maybe this weekend I'll stop by, you can cook since you brag about your skills so much," Ryann says with a hint of flirting right back. *Two can play this game, sir.*

"Oh you have no idea, but you might fall in love with me again, so watch yourself," Jameson teases.

"You will never change, good evening Mr. Clarkson."

"Good night Ms. Davis."

Jameson hangs up, he remembers his father telling him stories about the Pittsburgh Courier, and how important it was many years ago for the black community. It would be an honor to be featured in the paper. At one time *The Courier* was the largest circulated black newspaper in the country, and it was started right in Pittsburgh.

He felt good, things were coming into focus and he could feel the excitement throughout his body. As a child, he often struggled with confidence. He was tall and skinny growing up, he was often teased for having big feet, long arms and nothing else.

As is the case with many young boys, you have to cover the stench of fear by applying the deodorant of bravado. That was until he began to fill out, grow some hair on his face, and grow into his body. By the time Jameson was in high school, he developed quite a reputation for his shoes, his clothes and keeping a beautiful young woman by his side. At the time, he thought that was all you needed in life—some Jordans, Guess jeans and a cute girl...

Luckily making it through high school with no kids, he went to college and fumbled around through five years to earn his degree. He bounced around his hometown for a couple years, but grew tired and moved out west. He grew up, got married, had a daughter, got divorced, built and developed his own brand and now he was back.

Now, his bravado was real, total confidence flowed through his thoughts, comments and decisions. *But he still had one area that he kept tucked away as far and deep in his soul as possible.*

As he drove down Fifth Avenue, driving by his old High School Schenley, he realized he was still alone. He never really had a problem with being alone, he just loathed what he feared would be next, *being lonely*. That avenue he always feared, loneliness had come past his door a number of times in the past, and it eventually led to dark periods he would rather forget.

After his divorce, he felt lonely all the time. He would wake up, barely eat, do his show, come home and fall asleep, that was it.

He lost 15 pounds in a month, and was slipping into a space where he really didn't care about anything. His dream of having a family, seeing his daughter every day, having a best friend to love and to support was gone, and it crushed his spirit.

Thankfully, the love of his life, Zanita, looked at her father one day and said, "Daddy you look sick."

Jameson looked at himself in the mirror... his face was sunken in, his shoulders were not as broad, the glow of hope he exuded daily was gone, he was literally withering away. That was his bottom point, he could not allow himself to slip any further. Since that point he lived every day to the fullest and focused on being positive.

Jameson stopped downtown and walked to the point. The intersection of the three rivers, the Allegheny was in front, the Monongahela was to his back, and they formed the Ohio river off to the far left.

The air was cool and there was a slight breeze. It was an unusually clear night, many stars could be seen in the sky. The moon reflected off of the river, it was quiet and calm. When life as a teener or a young adult would cause some rift in him internally, Jameson would walk downtown and often end up on this same bench.

He enjoyed the tranquility of the rivers coming together, it was peaceful and relaxing to him. This place cleared his mind, allowed him to laugh, cry, or just sit by himself.

Tonight was for a different purpose... to refocus on what brought him here and the long term goals he set for himself. Jameson Clarkson was here for a rebirth, and he had to succeed.

He pulls his iPhone out and says, "Siri, text Adam Franklin..."

> Adam, this is Jameson Clarkson. Congratulations on your journalism career. I would be honored to set up an interview with you tomorrow, just tell me when.
>
> Me

> Your girl Ryann always comes through. Good to hear from you, my brother. Tomorrow is free for me, how about we meet at Pamela's in Squirrel Hill, grab some breakfast, and just chop it up, 10 am sound good?
>
> Adam

> Works for me, see you tomorrow at 10.
>
> Me

Jameson closes his text, locks his phone, sits back and breathes.

Yeah, this feels right, he thinks to himself.

8

Conversation With the Courier
(Part 1)

Jameson and Adam greet one another outside of Pamela's, a legendary Pittsburgh breakfast spot known for great food and small, overcrowded seating.

Adam Franklin wears black-framed glasses, stands around 6" tall, has put on a bit of weight since high school, wears a backpack, keeps notes in his small notebook, and types on his MacBook air.

He smiles a lot and has a great spirit about him. Jameson always admired that about him. No matter what was going on, he always seemed to be enjoying the moment--that is something he struggled with, even as an adult. Still, Adam had that down pact since they were young. Finally, the waitress comes by and takes their order.

"First of all Adam, it's good to see you and congratulations on your journalism career. It's impressive, I had no idea until last night you had done so much."

"I appreciate it, when Ryann called me I had to get an exclusive with you. It's cool you took it on short notice, you're about to blow up and I wanted to get you before you have 10 people to get through to even hear back from you."

They both smile and laugh.

"No, I won't ever be like that. I have a lawyer for contracts and things like that and otherwise I take care of everything else on my own. And Ryann she has a way with making things happen that's for sure."

"That's very true. Even back in high school she was like that and she's just got better over time. Whatever happened with the two of you anyway, I thought you'd be married with kid by now."

"Wasn't in the cards, at least to this point. So, how does this work?"

"It's just a simple Q&A session, we're going to do an overview of what you did out west, what brought you back home, talk about the future of your show and anything else that might come up. Just a simple conversation, mainly meant to highlight and give you a chance to get your voice out there before your new show starts. Sound good?"

"Absolutely, let's do it."

"I'll record our conversation but also take notes on my Mac and maybe even write some things down. I do have some questions I thought of before but I like to give some freedom for things that might come up."

Jameson nods in understanding.

"Jameson Clarkson, originally from Pittsburgh, left and came back home, it's like the Prodigal son from the Bible. What made you decide to come back after all these years?"

"Honestly it was a great opportunity. I felt that getting back east would be vital for the growth of the show and the brand itself. It gave me a chance to get back to my roots, this has and always will be home. There are things I missed about being home, and overall I felt like it would be a great change both professionally and privately as well."

"What challenges does moving back to your hometown present?"

"I think the biggest challenge for me personally is not to get complacent or stagnant. The show has to continue to grow and develop but never leave behind the chore of what got us here. We never want to leave the faithful listeners and followers that

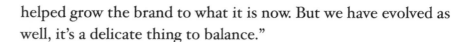

helped grow the brand to what it is now. But we have evolved as well, it's a delicate thing to balance."

"You've mentioned brand a few times now, what does the brand of Dr. Black Love mean and what does it mean to you personally?"

Jameson pauses to think for a moment.

"That's a great question, Dr. Black Love the brand itself stands for giving an honest and helping hand to a sector of the public that had never been catered to previously. Nobody really cared what people of color thought about love, relationships and the like before. Some of that has to do with stereotypes of black and brown men. All we do is have 10 kids and baby momma's running around. So, I hope the show is helping to shatter that bullshit myth and show that we are no different, we love, hurt, smile and cry just like everyone else."

"As far as what the brand means to me: To this point, it's a culmination of hours of work in front of a computer, making sure that I put my all into everything I do with the show-- rather it be on a post online, an Instagram live discussion, or simply being in front of a microphone for each show. I put my all into everything I do. I have been blessed to do this for a living, after doing it for free for a while. So I take great pride in what has been built."

"You know this is a world of back-stabbing, hating and being negative to everything. I see some of the comments left by people, I've seen everything from some men saying you're selling out men in general, people saying you have no business telling people what to do, etc. First of all do you read those comments at all?"

"I use to, when I first started especially. You want everyone to love you and what you are attempting to do. I would hang onto any negative thing that was said much more than the positive comments. Eventually I learned to not even look but it took a while."

"Who taught you that lesson Jameson?"

"Funny thing is I was taught that from my daughter Zanita, she was maybe 4-years-old. She's a beautiful little girl but there was another girl in her pre-school who would always tease her about her hair. One day we decided that she would not give that little girl the power over her by simply ignoring her, and what do you know... it worked! That made me reflect on myself, if I simply ignore the negativity because that will always be there, then I will not allow myself to be sucked into any dark places."

"Kids are amazing like that, I think if adults would look at the world through the lens of children, the world would be in a much better place."

"I agree 1,000% with you on that one," agrees Adam.

"So, you grew out west and now you are back east to expand and develop even more. Any insights into how the new show will be different?"

"I don't know exactly how much I can give away but I think that everyone will be pleased with the changes. We're going to be adding things to the show that expand on what we have done to this point. I want to be able to bring more listeners onto the show, more follow up stories because I feel like that adds validity and shows some vulnerability on our end. Believe it or not, I literally only speak to anyone on the show a few moments before we go live. We will continue to do that, just keeping things authentic," Jameson proudly says. He's worked hard to build this platform, one in which he is extremely proud.

"There is something that I don't feel like I have ever heard anyone ask you. What birthed Dr. Black Love?" Adam goes deeper.

"You trying to get deep on me huh, Adam?" Jameson smiles to himself and waits for a moment pondering on how to answer. He prides himself on being honest but is not as open with his own struggles at times.

"OK, so as with most people I have had my heart broken as well, multiple times. I have also broken women's hearts in the past also. I was going through a major crisis in my life at the time, I was going through a divorce, trying to figure out how to be a single father and share my daughter with her mother, new career had started and I was in some financial strains.

I had a lot going on. One day I was thinking and realized that I would not go speak to a professional about what I was sure was depression. And then I realized there are probably thousands of other people of color that felt the same way, mainly because most health care professionals are white. And I realized I could give advice based upon my life, having screwed things up enough and seen other people do it as well. And also seeing others succeed at the puzzle of love. We all want it, but there is no handbook on how to get it and keep it."

"That is so powerful and truthful. Love is the four letter word we all want but few actually get real love and even less keep it. What do you contribute to your brand's success?" Adam continues probing. Hoping to get the good goods.

"It's a different perspective, it's oftentimes raw and emotional, and I believe us allowing everyone to feel comfortable and have a voice helps. And to be quite honest, some of the letters or guests we have helps some people feel better about their own situations. Kind of like that Jerry Springer impact, you can look at someone else and say, *I'm not as bad as them*."

They both laugh.

"Where do you see Dr. Black Love being in five years?"

"Man, funny you ask that. If you asked me that 3 years ago when it started, I would have told you an exact answer. But the blessing and growth I have had has manifested itself in just staying in the moment, smelling the roses. I never did that before and had to learn to not focus so much on the future. You ignore so much to be thankful for in the present," Jameson says.

"So that means you kind of fly blindly with the direction of the brand?" Adam asks curiously.

"No, there are a couple directions I want to see things go in but they aren't set in stone. Life throws some curve balls at you

and you have to agile at times, if not you could miss a direction you should have went in."

"Do you have examples of how that has come to pass so far?"

"Well within 6 months of the show starting I was offered a chance to move to the Pacific Northwest, now if I was only thinking of the future and wanting to have a broader audience, I would have taken that offer. But I didn't and now less than two years later, we're on a bigger station, more markets and a much better contract," Jameson recalls.

"Nothing is wrong with that, Jameson. Before we conclude, is there anything you want to say to fans of Dr. Black Love and the feature coming to the Courier?"

"First, I want to say thank you for allowing me to grow and be here. Without fans and supporters that would not be possible. Second, the show will be starting very, very soon, so be on the lookout for that. Finally, keep those letters and emails coming in; that's what our show topics have been built on, and that will not change. We talk about what matters to you."

Adam sticks his hand out, and Jameson shakes his hand.

"Adam, I appreciate you."

"Thank you as well, Jameson."

The waitress places their breakfast in front of them, and they begin to eat.

9

Dear Dr. Black Love (Part 2)

Letter with Dr. Love's response on Instagram live...

"**H**ello everyone, once again it's Dr. Black Love coming to you live and in color. As always I want to thank everyone for their support, love and even the naysayers, I appreciate you.

There was a large number of people that want us to do this more often since the show is still in hiatus status, but we're so close to being on your airwaves every evening, so stayed tuned.

Today's letter is from a young man, which is always something I love to see. Men, we need help too, I know we're all tough, but no matter what you think, we can all use a supportive person on our side—that will only help you go farther. But anyway, let's get into this letter...."

"Dear Dr. Black Love, I have been a big admirer of your show for quite some time. Even back before you brought brothas on there to show our side of stories, I would listen to your show. Love the success of what you're doing and I wish you nothing but more success in the future.

For me, I realized that I need some help a long time ago, but I don't want to sit in front of some person I don't know or can't relate to. I'm hoping you can provide an impartial view of my situation. So here goes nothing....

For years I have 'dated' a few women at a time. And no, that doesn't mean sleeping with them, dating could be someone I go to dinner with occasionally and there is some interest, maybe a female or two that I am more serious with and spend more time with; but ultimately nothing serious for the last couple years. I wanted things to be easy, relaxed and not complicated; and to this point, I have been successful in keeping things that way.

Everyone I initially meet knows this is non-negotiable; if you're looking for your next husband to marry you within six months, I'm not that guy. Most women appreciate the honesty, I'd say maybe half think they can break me out of this cycle, but it doesn't work.

And I have had to have some very candid conversations with a few women to make sure they understand this is what I meant, and I am not changing for them or any other woman until I know I'm ready.

To give some context as to why I am here, I was in a long term relationship that ended on a sour note. We both kind of just grew tired of one another, I don't feel that ultimately we were a good fit, but we dated in our early twenties and grew up together but grew apart as well. When things ended, I took it kind of hard, and sort of bottled up and came out in this new phase of no real commitment and no expectations. Now that I read that, it sounds kind of weak, but this is where I am.

So now I have come to a crossroads... there is one young lady who seems different. Over two years of just kind of randomly dating, she's the only person that has caught my eye and heart, to be honest.

She's beautiful, both outside and more importantly inside. I have never met a more kind and level-headed person in my life. When I'm with her, my world just seems better. And more importantly to me, when I'm not with her, I want to be with her. That's an odd and scary feeling, one that I had to come to grips with, accept and not bolt the other way because I allowed myself to go there with someone.

Despite all that I have hesitations to fully immerse myself in this relationship. And for the life of me, I can't figure out why. I have some theories but they don't really make any sense. It's not like I want to be some major player forever but I also don't want to jump into something when I'm really not ready to do so.

Dr. Black Love, what the hell is wrong with me? Signed, Mr. Non-Committal"

"Mr. Non-Committal, I commend you on the courage to send that in. About 30% of the letters we receive are from men, which has grown tremendously over the last couple of years. So I get excited when I hear from men, just because I think society plays a major role in why we are scared to tell what's really inside of us, we're taught that isn't what men do, it makes us soft, a punk, whatever you want to call it. None of that is true and I try to help break down those barriers on this show and when we receive letters like this it helps with that process.

The first thing I picked up on was the fact you gave no real indication of any space after you and your long term girlfriend broke up. I always equate going through major trauma like losing someone you love or care about, whether it be romantically, platonically or even losing a family member to being in a car accident.

And what I mean by that is there are levels to going through trauma. If it's a bad car accident we could end up going away in an ambulance, or even worse dying unfortunately. Then there are minor fender benders on the other side of the spectrum. But most accidents are somewhere in the middle, and there are times we don't feel any impact from an accident until the next day, when the adrenaline goes away. Your neck or back will hurt, you're sore, most of us can relate to that in one way or another.

And in a relationship, when it ends, there is emotional trauma from that. Unfortunately most of us never really deal with it and we are still suffering from that damage in our next relationship and so forth. That's why I believe so many of us end up in the same type of relationship, just a new person with a different face but the same problems keep coming back up, over and over. We never got over our first accident, and now we're in accident number 7 and we're all screwed up.

So it seems that you went from ex to the next, and never really gave yourself to anyone but you probably never healed from your ex either. So my first piece of advice would be to examine why that relationship ended. Take responsibility for your part... now that's something that we hardly ever do. It's typically that crazy chick or that no-good man when we speak about our past relationships.

We rarely take into account what we did to make that relationship get to that point. It's not really all the other persons fault, normally we both play parts in causing a relationship to end. And that goes for friends and lovers equally. So my brother, take a moment and think back, take notes and figure out how you participated in the demise of that relationship, first.

Most of you know this but if not you'll hear it for the first time. I don't believe in that age old adage that if something is meant to be it'll be. I subscribe to the theory that God gives us opportunities, and it's up to us to seize them. They're similar but different. I always felt that believing the first motto would make you passive and indifferent to things in life. Kind of like waiting for a handout for everything, like the world owes you something and you're just going to sit around and wait for it to fall in your lap."

Jameson shrugs his shoulders.

"Now if you believe that, and it's worked for you to this point, more power to you. But for me, when I waited for things it always seemed like someone else would take it. So, me being me, I'm going to be the aggressor in most things and seize what I feel is meant for me.

The reason I bring that up is because I feel like you're possibly not seizing your moment sir. There isn't anything in this letter indicating this young lady is nothing but what you want in a woman. So why you gonna give that up? You're playing roulette with a beautiful young woman that seems to want you.

Men listen to me, typically when you have a good woman and you're honest about what you're going through, they'll ride with you. Women are loyal, sometimes to a fault of their own, but that's a story for another day.

So my second piece of advice is to complete step one and then figure out if you are fearful of being alone or being lonely. We all need to learn to be comfortable with being alone. When we jump around from person to person, it's often just to fill time.

Mr. Non-Committal, you need to do an assessment of yourself to see if you are dating all these women because of that fear. And if that's the case, nothing is wrong with that. But you have to fix that before you can go into a deep relationship.

Because if you never allowed yourself to heal and you've been filling time jumping from woman to woman, you're in the same place that you was two years ago.

Learn how to be without anyone, and not have a desire to call someone over, or go on a date, or sleep with a woman to help you temporarily feel better about yourself. Feel good about yourself first, and then you are the strong man that you should be, the strong man that a real woman will want to be with forever.

Now, finally don't let the fear of losing her prevent you from taking these steps. As a matter of fact, if you let her know why, if she's as good as you say she is, she won't go anywhere. Now she won't wait for years for you to grow but she'll support you and be there when you need her. So I encourage you to step outside of your comfort zone to grow.

Please let us know how your journey goes from this point forward. This is Dr. Black Love, and please remember that love only enters if the heart is willing, signing off Dr. Black Love."

10

Kolby Is Served

K olby is sitting in the office at the lounge; he is rarely in the office before 9 a.m. but today was a little different.

Although his office is always in some type of disarray, he enjoys the art of operating in a state of confusion. A 22-inch Cuban link chain is settled on his crisp white t-shirt; he has a black and white Jordan sweatsuit with a low cut pair of Air Jordan 1 low white university red sneakers.

He has lit a cigar but not even taken a tote of it yet, has a Bourbon on the rocks next to him, and ESPN plays lowly in the background on his 75-inch Samsung. Today's wristwatch is a

Benson Untitled Matte Black watch and a beaded black bracelet to match.

Kolby grew up poor; only he and his mother, who passed away when he was in college at Clark Atlanta. He took one day off, flew home for the funeral service, and went right back to Atlanta. His mother raised him to never worry about her; she was a hustler herself and never had time to raise a man concerned about anything outside of taking care of himself and being financially secure.

When he graduated from college, he started working in a small marketing firm but hated restraints because he felt owned by his manager. So he quit and vowed to never work for anyone again.

He took some of the money from his mother's passing away and his loan money from school to help start his empire. He now owns a couple of duplexes, a 4-unit apartment complex, his lounge, and a trucking business. But, he still wasn't satisfied; he considered himself a working hustler. The only thing that mattered was that he answered to no one and did what the hell he wanted to do.

Kolby's phone rings, and he answers...

"Paul, how you doing?"

Paul Romano was Kolby's lawyer; he was an Italian lawyer and played the part of a consigliere very well. He laid low, dressed in nothing but tailor-made suits, and most of the clients he represents are businessmen much like Kolby.

He grew up with a father who was sued many times while he owned a small grocery store. Seeing how ex-employees and strangers would try to take advantage, he decided he would protect business owners from frivolous lawsuits at a young age and has built a strong reputation for winning civil cases and amassed a small fortune in doing so.

"Kolby, what the hell is this about. I know you run off at the mouth a lot and talk shit to everyone including me but a civil lawsuit for wrongful termination and sexual harassment?! Do you even know this girl?" Paul says in disbelief that he is even having this conversation.

"Unfortunately I know her very well, Paul, that's part of the problem. We had some sort of relationship for a little while but I cut her off, she got lazy and stopped working, and we let her go, simple as that," Kolby replies, going over the facts in his head.

"Well it's never that simple, it's what she says and how bad she can make you look in front of a jury is what really matters. We've talked a thousand times about you not fooling with these girls, this is exactly why you don't swim in your own pool," Paul rolls his eyes. *Idiot.*

"I know, I can't say shit. The bitch got me it seems at this point," Kolby sounds helpless and his lawyer ain't offering no support to this point.

"Oh no, don't say that. We just have to figure out if you want to fight or settle. Fighting in civil court is different than criminal court as you know."

"Yeah, yeah I do. And either way it costs me money, so in the end I lose in that regard no matter what."

"If you view it that way, yes," says Paul, "There are many reasons people well off like yourself fight, mainly to clear your name and reputation. That way you don't lose what you have built over the past ten plus years of running clean businesses."

Kolby is quiet.

"Listen Kolby, I know this is really frustrating but you're going to be fine. Try not to let it bother you or impact anything else you have going on. It's Friday, get home early, relax and do something to take your mind off of this. Come in on Monday and we'll get a game plan together—I, I think you'll be in much better spirits."

Kolby takes a drink of his Bourbon.

"Yeah, that's a good idea. Paul, you have a great weekend."

"You do the same, don't get into anything stupid Kolby, we don't want anymore negativity to pop up and cloud the view on you."

"I got you."

Kolby hangs up the phone and finishes his drink.

His most valuable asset was him, and although he is often out of line, he does not make himself vulnerable to threats that can bring down his empire. To this point, he had done a great job of steering clear of the bullshit that can come as a young black man trying to build and not being an entertainer or an athlete.

He had no family members he was particularly close to, no 401K stored away somewhere. So he put his all into his businesses, and now he has a threat to his fortune and reputation. He will not go out without a fight, of course, but he has to make smart moves, and at a time like this, he needs his brothers around.

Kolby pulls out his phone and sends a text to the group chat with Jameson and Eero.

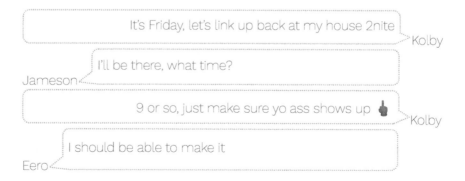

It's Friday, let's link up back at my house 2nite
Kolby

I'll be there, what time?
Jameson

9 or so, just make sure yo ass shows up
Kolby

I should be able to make it
Eero

Stop with that bullshit bruh, tell Mary you'll be home later and to give your ass a hall pass for the evening

Kolby

That's exactly why she don't like your fat ass now

Eero

You lucky I didn't take her off your hands in college

Kolby

Fuck outta here 😂😂😂😂

Eero

See y'all this evening

Kolby

//

Kolby's Castle

Kolby has always done things in a big way. He rented a stretch limo instead of a regular-sized limo or simply a car, all paid for in cash by himself for the prom.

When he graduated from college, as most graduates worried about that loan payment coming up in six months, he took a 2-week vacation to Turk's and Caicos. When he opened his lounge, he had a red carpet show, invited athletes, entertainers and invited several known DJs to keep the party going all night long.

Kolby's home was in the same line as his mindset coming up. He lives in Sewickley Heights, 5 bedrooms, 4.5 bathrooms, 5,500 square foot home. The house was gutted a few years previous to be more modern. The kitchen was white and gray with a matching island and four chairs, all new appliances; he had two entertainment areas in the basement, one had a 100-inch projection screen with a wrap-around couch for movies.

The other room had a pool table with an 80-inch television on the wall, a fully stocked bar, and surround sound throughout the basement in case you had to go to the bathroom and would miss a play on the Steelers winning drive for that Sunday.

The master bedroom had an old-school clawfoot bathtub, shower, bidet, and a urinal. Two equally huge closets, one was filled with designer sweatsuits and the other with suits, dress shoes, all of which he hardly ever wears, but just in case.

Jameson always thought the house was too big for someone with no wife or kids, but again, this was Kolby. This was always how he had envisioned himself living, and he was doing it. They loved when they could hang out and just kick it like when they were younger and didn't have responsibilities.

Jameson pulls up to the house; Eero's vehicle is already there. Jameson walks right in without knocking as Kolby never locks the door for some reason.

"You don't know how to knock?" says Kolby from the kitchen.

"I'll knock when your ass learn how to lock the door. What you gonna do shoot and ask questions later?" exclaims Jameson as he walks into the kitchen and gives dap to them both.

"You know this fool has a handgun in every fucking room right?" as Eero opens a drawer and lifts a 9mm Ruger out of a random drawer.

"Listen, I told you all a million times, I don't carry outside of my house cause I talk too much shit and I don't want to do something stupid. But if some fool run up in my house, he's gonna get it with multiple bullet holes, I promise you that much," Kolby says rocking back and forth pointing his hand in a gun motion as if he's shooting the perpetrator.

"Well that brings up a good discussion...." Jameson, as he often does when they get together, enjoys the sparring of great discussions. He will often take the opposite side of Eero and Kolby just to keep the debate going.

"I know a few black men in similar situations like Kolby and they seem to have a similar mindset."

"Yeah that's cause you have jealous ass, lazy assholes that would rather try to run in your spot and take instead of working hard and getting the same shit," exclaims Kolby.

Eero chimes in also, "No question, I don't have no 5,500-square foot home like Mr. Richardson, but we got a nice spot as well of course. And I definitely have a well stocked fire arm collection, and Mary knows how to fire each one of them."

Jameson explains, "I'm not trying to say that anything is wrong with it, or for either of you to justify having armory in either of your homes. I was speaking more about the mindset or deeper reasoning behind it."

Kolby cut's him off... "Look before you get into your diatribe about whatever you want to discuss tonight, your black ass want a drink? Cause I'm gonna need another since you starting this talk show host shit already."

"What the fuck ever bro, you know these discussions are amazing and you're just jealous you don't think of them first."

"What your ass want?"

"Give me a henny-n-coke," says Jameson.

Eero says, "I don't know how black people drink that shit, Hennessy is some nasty shit. But y'all keep them in business. I don't ever see white people drinking that neither."

"I guess that's why your ass don't drink it then, since you ain't black all of a sudden, Mr. Williams," as Kolby holds up his glass towards Eero in a toasting fashion.

"I'm black and have enough courage to not drink some nasty shit just cause everyone else do," Eero shoots back.

"Eero, shut your shit up, you eat more stereotypical black shit than anyone I know. You eat chitterlings, only eat greens with pork in it, you eat everything on a pig," Jameson says, getting louder with each word.

"I like what I like, and I don't like what I don't like."

"Let's head down to the basement fellas," says Kolby, and he leads them downstairs.

After playing pool, more drinks, and laughs, the conversation turns back to the discussion upstairs after an hour or so.

"All jokes aside Kolby, why you have so many guns in here?" Eero asks.

Kolby steps away from the pool table and thinks to himself for a moment.

"To be honest, it's out of paranoia. It don't matter the level we get to as black men, we always gotta watch out for someone trying to bring us back to where we came from. Now in the matter of a gun, it's literally to protect my life, if someone comes in here they aren't coming to wish me good luck, they coming to take my shit, my life or both. I won't have time to run to some damn vault and hope nothing happens."

"But what has happened for you to go to the extreme, and forgive me for calling it that, but to me, having a piece in each room is a little extreme," Eero states matter of factly, knowing he can have real conversations with these two gentlemen here, if no one else.

"Nothing has happened, but you never know. I didn't have anything growing up, no Dad, no real family besides my mom.

So I worked really hard for everything, not saying you two haven't. But I won't let someone walk up in here and take that from me, I just can't do it. Only like four or five people, including you two, know where I actually live. I drive a new way home every night, just in case," Kolby shares something he has never really said out loud before.

"I used to worry about that as well. Like being known in the public puts a bulls eye on your back. I can't imagine the shit that a celebrity goes through, or some star athlete. Every day someone is looking to get in your pockets, how can you trust anyone?" says Eero.

"Biggie said it best, mo' money, mo' problems. I have to keep all my ducks in a row professionally and personally. All it takes it one thing to bring a brotha down, we don't get three, four chances like these white people out here."

Jameson chimes in, "So you feel that threatened or that much of a target?"

"Yes!" Kolby don't get why they don't get it.

"From who?" asks Jameson.

Kolby puts down his pool stick, walks over to his desk, and hands Jameson the paperwork showing he is being sued.

"That shit right there, that's not a threat on my life but a civil trial puts my entire reputation and name on the line. So from all sides I have to protect myself, at all times bro. That's just how it is."

Jameson reads over the paperwork and hands it to Eero.

"Damn, does she have a case?" Eero asks, looking over the paperwork thoroughly.

Kolby takes a long swig from his drink and pauses, "We fooled around a bit, then I cut it off."

Jameson and Eero both shake their heads in disbelief.

"Yeah I know it was stupid, and I literally have never put myself in that position before. I tried to let someone in and this is the thanks I get, that's why I don't fool with these bitches. I just stick and move, and keep it going," Kolby bitterly blurts out. "They tryna stick me for my paper!" Quoting Biggie just seems appropriate at this moment.

"Well this shit won't go away unless you pay her," says Jameson.

"I'm not paying her shit, fuck that." Screams Kolby as he aggressively puts down his drink.

"From a public relations standpoint you might want to think about it Kolby."

"Eero, that's basically admitting I fired her because we didn't work out, whose to say the next host or dispatcher at the truck business won't just do the same?" asks Kolby.

"You never know but if you fight this, it'll be more expensive, you could still lose, take a hit on your reputation, and the only thing that's changed is your size of your bag," Jameson responds.

Kolby takes a seat on the couch and is silent.

"We got you bro, whatever you need just let me know. You know we got some people that in certain situations are just a call away." Jameson says in support.

"No question, I just don't know what to do."

"You still have that Italian lawyer, Romano or whatever his name is," asks Eero.

"Hell yeah," responds Kolby.

"You can't get any better in the city, what did he say?" asks Eero.

"We're gonna meet Monday, that's why I called you both over here, just to tell you both and to take my mind off of the shit."

"Well we're doing a horrible job of that," says Eero.

"This is real life, this ain't some low level shit. We got you, no matter what. Just don't drink yourself into doing something stupid," says Jameson as he picks up the bottle of Tito's vodka that Kolby has been drinking most of the night.

"That's light weight shit there," Kolby says as he laughs at Jameson's gesture.

"I'll be good... this won't get me down just another hurdle, it'll work itself out. Jameson, what's going with the show? When the hell is it starting?"

"Monday afternoon... I'm nervous too."

Kolby and Eero look at one another in astonishment.

"Yeah I know I don't typically get nervous but this first show is big. There are some changes, that make the show better but it's not like it was before. There's a new time slot and I have a fine ass co-host now named Keisha...."

"Jameson, please don't be fucking this girl..." says Kolby.

"Damn, I don't fuck every girl," Jameson replies.

Kolby and Eero stare at Jameson with an incredulous look.

"Kolby, really in your situation you have nerve to talk. And Eero, you only had sex with like two girls in your entire life." Jameson fires back at them both.

"None of that has anything to do with you and the extremely long list of conquests you have on your board," Eero fires back.

"To answer what your both implying, no I'm not and will not. However, I saw Ryann the other day anyway, maybe that'll work out."

"Here we go, I was wondering when it was going to come up, Ryann, just leave her alone." Says Kolby.

"Why?" asks Jameson.

"This is a re-run we've all seen before is all I'm saying."

"You never know Kolby, I might just give it another shot."

"I sincerely hope not," says Kolby.

"Back to the show, cause I don't want to hear anything else about Ryann." Says Eero.

"Whatever... The show has some changes but it'll be dope. I'm happy with the way things have turned out, and we'll get it going Monday."

Kolby pours another drink.

"Here's a toast... To Jameson Clarkson, finally bringing his talents back home to where it started, here's to much success," says Kolby.

"And we'd be remised if we didn't toast to you as well Kolby," says Jameson.

"Absolutely, to get through the drama and come out even better," says Eero.

They all toast each other and take another drink.

12

It's Showtime!

The last segment of the first show in the new Dr. Black Love era.

"So, Dr. Black Love, how do you feel about the first episode to this point?" Keisha asks as she shuffles paper across the desk, tidying up her area a bit.

"Today's show has been great. We've done it all, we've done some incoming calls, read a few letters that has been stock-piling over the last month or so since the show has been away... it's been great. What do you think?" Jameson says and throws the question back at his new co-host.

"I agree, I think that the audience is pleased with the changes and they're loving how things are moving. Just looking at things online out there, overall it's extremely positive."

Jameson interrupts, "So you're saying that the people like me and love you?"

They both laugh.

"Nope, not at all. Things look good in the social media space, as far as reactions from people overall. You always have naysayers but that comes with the territory."

"Without question," he says.

"So, we are in our final segment and we're going to do something new today. Are you ready?" Keisha throws in a curve ball, seeing if Jameson will take the bite.

"Let's do it. But we have to explain what we're doing of course," Jameson agrees, ready for the challenge. *This could be fun*.

"Alright, so people there are two people that we deal with on this show: Dr. Black Love, and then there is Jameson. Dr. Black Love is the omniscient one of love, the one that we all have come to admire, trust and look up to. Then there's Jameson... The thirty something year old, often single, so-called never lonely person that we don't know much about. So, I decided that from time to time, we would get to know this person as well. Now tonight, we'll let Jameson have an open mic to answer a topic," Keisha says into the microphone.

"Right, and I have no idea what Keisha, my co-host is going to ask. No idea at all, and this is me answering as I would if I was speaking to one of my closest friends," says Jameson.

Keisha adds, "And if anyone wants to know why, I thought it would be nice to just hear from you. So people can see how Jameson works, and not just Dr. Black Love. You ready?"

"Shoot your shot Keisha."

"So, what is one of the rules that Jameson abides by when it comes to dating?" Keisha says, looking Jameson in the eyes.

"Good question," Jameson starts but stops to think.

"OK... so I don't have a ton of rules that are absolutes. I think you can short change yourself or a potential great fit if you are too hard-lined with things. For instance, I know men that won't date a woman within a certain height or if she doesn't have this certain length of hair or something like that...."

"So you don't have any superficial things that you grade women by and eliminate them immediately?" asks Keisha, pushing the envelope slightly.

"You're trying to get me in trouble, but I won't let you," says Jameson smiling.

"I apologize, please continue...." Keisha says with a slight giggle.

"Apology not accepted," says Jameson.

They both laugh.

He continues, "So, having said that I do have one general rule that I follow but it's kind of a secret. However being as though I am as single as I have ever been in life, I will let the world know because that's what we do on this show. I have a six-month rule for dating."

"Six-month rule in dating... what the hell does that mean?" Keisha is curious now and sits up in her chair.

"Basically it means I will not date someone over six months," Jameson states bluntly. *I can't believe I just told them that.*

"What's so significant about six months?" asks Keisha.

"I'll explain why I have the rule or what made me develop it and that'll explain why that time period is so significant."

Standing behind the boards on the other side of the glass, Abraham gives two thumbs up in a show of support for both Keisha and Jameson.

Jameson gives a thumbs-up back to him.

"When you first start dating, the first month or two is literally getting to know someone of course. Like Chris Rock said you only meet their representative, you only see what they want you to see. After that most people kind of break down or even before that and show their real self.

So, at that point you really can access if this is someone that you want to invest in long term after that. Everything is typically better the first few months of a relationship. You don't take the other person's time for granted, you smile when they call or text, you actually listen to what they're talking about on the phone, you care about what they want to eat or what they don't like.

Then typically around six months, the complacency sits in. The parameters of the relationship have been established and you are basically set in your ways for however long you are with that person. So typically we fail at relationships as I always say so it doesn't work itself out, then we rinse, dry off and repeat with another person.

The biggest difference between myself and most people is that I don't waste those extra six months to a year or even more going through the minutia of a dead end relationship."

Keisha sits there for a moment.

"I must say, that is pretty interesting. So you feel all relationships should be six months or less?" she asks.

"Nope, I never said that. This is all about me, that's what this segment is about."

"So why do you encourage people throughout your entire time to seek love?"

"Love is so important to everyone, I just have been through enough right now that over the past few years, I decided to guard myself from the hurt of things not working... the hurt, the pain that all that causes. It was too much for me to deal with so I closed myself off from it," Jameson shines in his element of speaking truth.

"Someone really hurt you Dr. Black Love."

"It goes both ways, rarely is it just one person hurting the other, there's blame on both sides. It's not just one incident, it's a lifetime of it all building, most of it you get over, there are always fragments that you can never fully get rid of."

Abraham holds a fist to them both to indicate the time is running out.

"I must admit I did not expect to hear anything like that from you sir," Keisha says.

"You'll learn I am full of surprises as we continue on this journey together," Jameson smiles and nods at Keisha.

"My people, we are very grateful for the opportunity to be with you today. I, for one as your only co-host, appreciate your willingness to bring me in and trust me."

"Keisha, great job today, you are definitely an asset to what we're building. People, we could not do this without you. Thanks to everyone for your patience while we build and grow for the future. Please tell your family members, your friends, your ex's, anyone and everyone about what we're doing here. And please remember, love only enters if the heart is willing, signing off, Dr. Black Love."

Abraham walks into the studio.

"That was a hell of a show, I must admit. Social media, the phone lines, everything is just hot right now. What do you think Jameson?" He looks at the shining star.

"It went well, I loved the last segment also even though I don't deal with ambiguity well, I think people will react to it if nothing else. And that will keep things going, just hope some people aren't turned off by it."

Abraham responds, "We can manage that, I recall my parents always saying *do as I say, not as I do* or whatever that is... same thing here. Just because you aren't seeking to be with someone for the next fifty years doesn't mean you can't help someone that is in that situation. You just aren't yourself."

"How do you feel Keisha?" asks Jameson.

"I feel good, I am still blown away by your answer. There are so many questions I have...."

"I think we should do that daily, people love the show because of you but they don't know you, the real Jameson so peeling back some of those layers but not too many will only add to the legend," explains Abraham.

"Well I can ask you questions for about two years based off that response."

Jameson chuckles to himself.

"That's why we do that segment last, to keep people's minds turning and tuning in tomorrow and the next day and so forth."

Abraham and Keisha both nod in agreement and begin to gather their belongings.

Jameson's phone vibrates, and he picks it up. He sees her name on the screen and smiles.

Ryann — Interesting show tonight

Me — 😳

Ryann — I need to come talk 2u

Me — You mean come over to MY place?

Ryann — Yes fool, what else would I mean?

Me — OK, I'll see u there in an hour

Ryann — C u then

13

Night With Ryan

Jameson is sitting on his couch, sipping on Bourbon, Miles Davis' *Kind of Blue* is playing in the background, and he is looking outside of his floor-two-ceiling windows.

His view is spectacular; his new place sits right across from downtown, with the waterfront of the Allegheny River below. Tonight is a peaceful night downtown, no ball game, no shows, just buildings overlooking the streets, the warm air is blowing, and the occasional car driving by.

The air is thick and humid, the sky is dark and beautiful, the moon reflects off the water, there is a calm that is rare for a city at night that is soothing to his soul. He has been in his place for almost six weeks, yet he has never really sat down and taken it all in—too busy running to this meeting or to see this person, he is content with his new start back home.

Ryann has always been special to him. Without question, she was his first love, at least what you know love to be as a teenager and young adult. He has never subscribed to the notion that you can only love one person, but he has always felt something special for her.

When they ended their relationship, he swore he would never feel the same way about another woman, and to this point, his prediction has been accurate. Yes, he's been married, conceived a child in that union, but that was not the same.

Ryann allowed Jameson to be Jameson, something that no one else could come close to doing. Yet, he never felt that he could ever get back to that moment or, better yet, even create another moment in time with her. Now fate has somewhat brought them back together, and he would love to see where things go from here.

There is a knock at the door, which startles Jameson. He was rather enjoying his mental break. *She's here.* He walks to the door, looks through the peephole.

"How did you get in the building?" he asks.

"Just open the door please," Ryann quickly responds.

Jameson obliges and lets Ryann in; he takes her coat, and she grabs his drink, walks over, and takes a seat.

"Are you thirsty, I can get you your own drink Ryann."

"No, I'll just drink yours."

Jameson sits next to her.

"So, why did you want to talk to me?"

Ryann takes a sip and puts the drink down.

"I listened to your show tonight, and it was good. But the last segment, I'm not so sure about that part."

"What do you mean?"

"Are you just playing games with me? This rule that you arbitrarily came up with about six months, like we spend time with one another, we hang out, we go out to eat, is this all fun and games for you?" Ryann needs answers before she gets too invested in his return home saga.

"Not at all, I am enjoying every minute of the time we spend together," Jameson chimes in with that reassuring tone.

"Then what is it Jameson, you can't talk out of both sides of your damn mouth. If what you said is true today, then we have what three months left together, then you'll ignore my ass too?"

"You're different, you're not some random female, you're Ryann...."

Ryann is not paying attention and completely ignores his statement.

"You claim to always speak the truth to your audience, blah, blah, blah... But that is not the Jameson Clarkson that I know. He would never just give some beautiful female he is interested in a measly 180 days and just be done with her, forever. That is not you at all."

Jameson pauses for a moment, realizing that Ryann is totally ignoring his previous comment, "Well, you don't know me over the last few years because that's exactly what I tell everyone, the first time we go out. It'll be the best six months of your life but it won't go any longer."

"And these women, still go out with you?" Ryann asks with a look of disbelief.

"Absolutely, there's something about women that makes them want to show a man that they can change them or they simply think I'm full of shit; but either way, nobody has turned and ran away to this point."

Ryann shakes her head and looks out the window.

"You never said that to me."

"When?"

"Anytime we've seen each other since you came back," Ryann recalls.

"Of course not, you aren't some chick, you're Ryann. You've always been special to me, believe it or not."

"It's not that I don't believe you, it's just you never could consistently follow it up. You always did some stupid shit, always."

"I was young... and stupid... and horny... and whatever else you want to call it."

"What do you want from me Jameson?"

"Nothing," he says plainly.

"Everyone wants something, rather it be sex, to talk, something," Ryann probes for answers that satisfy her insecurities.

"I love being around you, I always have. Even when I was too young to articulate how I craved being with you. I can't put my mind around why but you literally soothe my soul. I could be 20 feet from you and still my heart would be content at just being able to see you. Nobody has ever made me feel that way, ever."

Ryann gets up and walks over to the windows, and turns around.

"I don't want to go through all of this with you again and end up being hurt, Jameson. If you're that cold to someone you just met, why wouldn't you be even less caring about me?"

Jameson walks over to her.

"I would never do that to you, you're special to me."

"I guess time will tell."

Ryann walks to the couch and sits, finishes her drink, and places it on the end table.

"Come sit next to me please."

Jameson obliges and takes a seat.

"You hurt me really bad back then, and for a while I swore I would never speak to you again in life. Seeing you brought up a lot of things inside me that I never really dealt with. I know you're special to me as well and if we do this I need to know you're all in, not half of you, not almost all of you... I need all of you. And most importantly, I need to be the only one."

"I can do that, but are you really ready for that?" Jameson asks, being cautious even though she's saying all of the right things right now.

"I don't know if either of us are but I would love to try."

"Me too," Jameson eagerly agrees.

"So where do we go from here?"

"I don't know, let's just take it one day at a time and see what happens."

"Please love me the right way this time."

"I will... Can I lay on you?" Jameson shoots his shot.

Ryann nods in agreement and lays down on the couch. Jameson lays between her legs and on her stomach.

Throughout their years together, they would often fall asleep in this same position. But tonight was not a night for sleeping; they both were on the verge of giving each other the badge for hurting one another. They had both tucked away their hurt for so long, they only felt it could be healed by being together once again. Jameson feared running away too early, while Ryann feared she would be left again to see the man she loves with another woman. Yet, in this very moment, it felt good to hold one another again, to feel one another's heartbeat, to embrace one another.

Jameson was able to take a deep breath, knowing that he was with the one person in the world that had never failed him. He trusted Ryann with every fiber in his body, and outside of Zanita, he did not care about another person more on the face of the earth. So he lays there with his face between her breasts, closes his eyes, and just breathes.

Ryann loved Jameson's body and mind. She always felt safe with him, as if no matter what happened, he would always take care of her. She saw his mind blossom from a teenager to a young adult, while his mind exploded as he learned more about the world and his unique talent within it. Finally, she closes her eyes and allows herself to feel his strength, and let go in his arms.

They both lay without saying another word and fall asleep in one another's arms.

14

Preparing for Battle

E ero was always an early riser; today, he woke up around 5 a.m. and immediately drove down to the office.

It was time to prepare for the election, and he had to be on point with everything, his legacy and career to this point depending upon him winning, and he was determined to do just that.

Eero is a workaholic; he puts his all into the two things he cares about the most, his job and family. There was not much else he cared about nor much time for anything in between. He worked diligently in his office, scribbling notes on a notepad

that only he could decipher. The whiteboard had multiple ideas written out in numerous colored markers, and he had already drunk two cups of coffee before 8 a.m.

He won his initial election to become the City Controller by sheer popularity; he ran as a native of the City, a successful businessman who would help steer the ship of the cities finances the right way, slam dunk. Since he took control of the office, he has done an excellent job protecting the City from wasting money, which is his main priority. He has cleaned up some of the wasteful spendings by specific departments within the City and clarified the division of contracts.

However, this is Pittsburgh, a city that is still very much divided within neighborhoods by one simple factor, the color of your skin. Outside of the occasional sprinkle here or there, you can almost guess where someone lives simply by their ethnicity or race.

Eero has never backed down from these challenges, yet they play a factor in how he has to approach every aspect of his campaign. From how he markets himself and his family to how much time he spends in various neighborhoods. Quite frankly, he has to win a good percentage of the vote from white voters. He has never had an issue with intermingling in the circles necessary to succeed in any area he has in life.

Politics, though is a different animal, people often sell their souls to gain a powerful endorsement, all in the name of winning. He hates to lose, but he does not like to become someone's bitch in the process.

Eero stops writing and pauses; he could still hear Mary's words recently about not losing. He had never thought about not losing, his mind has always been focused on the W, but now she had thrown some doubt into his usual sangfroid demeanor.

Mary was right; his competition did have several areas in his favor; he was white and single. He already knew his gameplay; he was older than Eero, he technically had more experience by default as one would expect in dealing with someone almost ten years his senior.

With all that being said, Eero was still confident he could and would win. He would play this election by standing on his body of work over the last four years. As always in these publicly elected seats, he had to be squeaky clean, and he was as clean as they came. He has been well-schooled in the art of playing his cards well, and he knew what buttons to push to get the job done.

His staff was beginning to come into the room now. The plan was in place; he just needed everyone to stay in their lane, execute and operate efficiently. The war was about to begin for his career, and he felt possibly even his marriage.

The campaign would not be turned into some assault on his opponents flaws or missteps in his career. Even though those could be exposed and quickly propel him to victory, that would also open the door for those tactics being used with or without evidence against him.

He did not feel that that would help him in any political arena; that is an uphill battle he would instead leave alone. Being dirty, grimy, and unethical is a road he never wanted to be on, or even close to.

Just a Little Talk

Jameson is working on his laptop and he receives a text message. *Hmmmm, Mary? What does she want*, he ponders as he opens his text message app.

> Jameson, I need 2 talk 2u

Mary

> Hey Mary, about what?

Me

> Obviously if I wanted 2 text u about it, I would have done so already... don't have a lot of time, my mom is watching the kids for a couple hours...

Mary

Where do you want to meet?
Me

I'm downstairs already
Mary

How the hell do you know where I live?
Me

U are best friends with my husband, u do know this right?
Mary

Touché. I'll buzz you up.
Me

thx
Mary

Jameson opens the door, they give each another a hug, and Mary walks in.

Mary and Jameson have a long history together. Since elementary school, they have known one another, but they became good friends in high school once Mary started dating Eero. They have always maintained a good relationship; Mary befriended Camryn and was one of the few people visiting over the years. They had not spoken as much since Jameson and Camryn divorced, but Jameson knew if she was coming to see him, then something was up.

"Mary, nice to see you again. I haven't seen or heard much from you since I got back home," Jameson breaks the silence.

"I wanted you to get settled, get your place together... this is very nice Jameson, that big money from the radio station is paying off I see," Mary says looking around the home in approval. "Nice."

"Here you go with these jokes, I got divorced remember, I got bills out the ass now. But I do like this place, the open space is good for me. Speaking of which, I don't hear from you much, I guess that's because you're on Team Camryn?"

"I'm on Team Z..."

"Oh, so you gone speak to Zanita but you don't speak to her father that you've known for decades... that makes sense," Jameson says.

He walks over to the refrigerator and grabs bottled water, "Would you like one?"

"No thanks," Mary says.

He motions towards the dining room table and they both take a seat, Mary placing her purse on the table in front of her.

"Jameson, I didn't know what to do. I loved you two as a couple, I don't know all that happened but I do know that I lost a friend and we're in an odd space."

"That's because of you though, you don't speak much. When I come over to see the kids, you kind of dart out. What did I do to you?"

"I just don't know what to say... You didn't do anything to me. I am just confused on how to act. Can I be friends with both of you still?"

"Camryn and me... you really would have to think about who you would chose if you had to? Wow, that's interesting Mary."

"I want to be friends with you both. I like her, we grew close over the years, but I am not picking sides. Maybe I'm being selfish, I don't know."

"I get it, I just don't like that our relationship fell off like that. Things didn't work out but I'm still the same person who had braces in middle school, had that awkward haircut the first day of high school... come on, you was like my sister. I just miss the interaction, we all fun together but that doesn't have to stop because Camryn won't be around anymore," Jameson says to his old friend.

"I apologize, I'll do better. But your ass better do better as well. I won't get into it, but Camryn told me a few things...."

Jameson rolls his eyes, "If you came over here for all that then you'll be here for more than two hours."

"No, no I didn't. I'm nervous about Eero."

"Nervous... Nervous about what?"

"The election..." Mary admits. She always could talk to Jameson. He made her feel heard.

"He's gonna beat that clown, polls are showing good numbers."

"Yeah but that won't last."

"How do you know?" Jameson asks.

Mary tilts her head and looks at Jameson.

"Your father, of course. He's like the black hand in the Mafia, he knows everything but you never see him. Well if he knows then I'm sure he knows how to fix it."

"That's why I need you, Eero won't take his help. And if he waits too long then it might be too late," Mary pleads. If anyone can talk some sense into her stubborn husband, it's this guy.

"So you need my help to nudge him to listen I'm assuming."

"Eero listens to you, at least he'll consider what you have to say. With me he just blows me off now," Mary says defeatedly.

"That doesn't seem like him at all. What else is going on then?" Jameson asks.

"I don't know, maybe you can help us since you help so many people now on your show."

"Me help the perfect couple?... hell I used the two of you as an example on the show!"

"Falling in love is not the issue, staying in love and making it grow is very hard. And sometimes you lose sight of who you are, what you are as a couple, things get off track. And when that happens unless both people help get things back, it'll never be the same," Mary speaks from a place of her truth.

"Shouldn't the goal be to get better, not be the same?"

"I'd take the same over where we are now."

"Eero hasn't mentioned anything out of the ordinary to me. Just normal like shit that everyone goes through."

"He can throw himself into his work, into his campaign, outside of the babies I don't have much to throw myself into."

"So is this about you wanting a career, your marriage or both?" Jameson asks.

Mary thinks to herself for a moment.

"I think that I need him at home more, I want our marriage to be stronger and I want to do more than be at home. I guess I want it all, which is probably impossible."

"I don't know if that's true, there are couples that do it all the time. But my only question is what did you all agree to? It might be kind of hard for him to change the way things are now if you change course at this moment," Jameson is in his element.

"Something has to give Jameson, I can't keep on this path forever. I'm not happy, simple as that," Mary says, but really can't believe she said it out loud.

Jameson walks away while looking down at the ground. He's very perplexed as to how to handle this conversation. He understands both sides of the coin and loves both of them, so he would prefer not to be put into the middle, too late for that now.

"Mary why did you put me in the middle of this?"

"Because I know you'll help, who else would I speak to?... crazy ass Kolby?" she laughs.

Jameson smiles in agreement, "Yeah, I guess between the two of us, Kolby would agree with that."

Jameson comes back to sit at the table.

"So I'll speak to him, I don't know when but I will. Just don't do anything drastic, like run off with the kids, move out or something. He's pretty stressed already."

"I know how to play my position but I will not be unhappy and play it for long. Talk to your boy please."

Jameson closes his eyes and nods.

Mary stands up and grabs her purse.

"Thank you Jameson, I appreciate you."

"I know, I love you both which is why you know I'll do all I can to help."

Mary nods in agreement and walks out.

Jameson closes his eyes, and his alarm goes off on his phone. Showtime in an hour, he needs to get into the studio.

He grabs his keys and heads out.

16

Call From Zanita

Jameson is driving past PNC Park and heading over the 6th Street bridge when he receives a call from Camryn.

Not good timing at all, Jameson thinks to himself. So typically, he keeps his contact with Camryn to a minimum. Although Zanita has her own iPad to FaceTime her, he usually texts Camryn if something needs to be discussed.

Not that he avoids conversations, he just prefers to keep them at a minimum and only speak if absolutely necessary. Right now, trying to get into the studio on time to prep for today's show, the conversation with Mary is still fresh on his mind. He just wasn't in the mood for the typical inconsequential conversation that could be brewing on the other side of the line.

Things were not always so jaundiced between the two of them. The first couple of years of their relationship were actually quite good. Camryn was like a breath of fresh air to him. She was free-spirited, easy to get along with, and open-minded. From most of the women he had dated, she was very unique in that respect. Perhaps it was her upbringing in a different environment than he was from. Her parents were pretty well off; she went to a prep school, her parents paid for college, and she did not grow up with any worries at all.

Jameson grew up in what most would consider an extremely hostile environment, he had a lot of love in his home, but outside of those four walls, there was a lot of hurt, anger, and frustration in the streets. That led to most battles he saw in various forms: arguments, name-calling, fighting, gun battles, and death. Those two worlds collided all the time in their relationship and caused many rifts between them.

In most relationships, there are underlying issues that are rarely discussed but cause massive explosions. The contradiction in their upbringing had caused them to be two very different people as adults. Jameson was very hard-core on the outside, sparring to keep anyone who tried to come close to him at a distance. Camryn, to the contrary, was very inviting and wanted someone close to her at all times. Instead of these unique characteristics of the two bringing them closer, they tore their relationship apart. Neither of the two knew it at the time, but their greatest strength was also their greatest weakness when it came to them both.

They did love each other, but they reached a tipping point caused by too many years on the merry-go-round of not dealing with problems, covering the stench with fake promises of changing. These gifts sit in a closet or on a coffee table and making love that lasts for some time but ultimately puts you right back at the same place where you started. And without the proper work being put in, no relationship grows; it only dies a very slow death.

With all these thoughts running through his head, he finally answered the phone...

"Yes Camryn," Jameson says dryly.

"I didn't think you was going to answer," Camryn says shockingly. She was prepared to leave a voice message like every other time.

"You know my show starts soon and I need to be in the studio soon so why are you calling me?"

"But you aren't."

"No, that's because your friend Mary came by to speak to me and just left not too long ago."

"Oh, nice. How is she doing?"

"She's good... Camryn, what do you want?"

"Oh yeah... We need to talk but your daughter wants to speak to you," Camryn calls out, "Z, your dad is on the phone now."

Shuffling from the phone being passed.

"Hi daddy," says Zanita.

Jameson smiles, something about her voice just lights up his world. It's incredible how hearing your child's voice can do that.

"Hello my love, how are you today?" Jameson's voice softens.

"I'm good but I miss you," Zanita says sadly.

"I miss you so much, you have no idea. How was school today?" Jameson changes to subject hurriedly.

"It was good Mrs. Patterson said I was very good today. And I wore my new shoes you got me, they're so pretty. Mommy says I can't sleep in them for some reason tonight."

"Well that's probably a good idea Z, you don't want to sleep with shoes on your bed, but you can wear them again tomorrow. I am glad that you like them."

"They're so pretty daddy."

"Just like you sweetheart," Jameson smiles. This is a pleasant surprise right before the show.

"When are you coming back home?" Zanita asks.

That question stings Jameson to the core. He immensely misses his daughter, and this move has been harder on him than he could have imagined. He has everything in place, his career, his family, but he needs his daughter. They made an arrangement, and he has to stick to it, but it hurts nonetheless. Jameson begins to tear up but pulls himself together.

"I'll be home soon sweetheart. Can you put your mother back on the phone? I will call you to say goodnight on your iPad like I always do."

"OK, love you daddy."

Zanita hands Camryn the phone.

"Yes Jameson," Camryn says dryly. She doesn't care to speak to him that much either.

"How is she doing?"

"She's doing pretty well, she asks about you all the time. She wants to listen to the show every night, she constantly talks about you."

"That's my little girl."

"What you need to be asking is how I'm doing?"

"I'm not sure why I should be asking you that but how are you doing?"

Jameson pulls into the garage to park for the show.

"This is a lot to handle. Having her all the time is tough, I don't have much help out here."

"I understand that, I told you I had some people that could help with Z, but you told me you didn't want help. And we agreed to a year before she comes out here full-time."

"I know that but I don't know, I just don't know," Camryn says.

Over the years, Jameson has learned how to handle Camryn in these moods. The difference was he is now over 2,000 miles away and can't come to save her or his daughter in the blink of an eye. For years he would come to get Zanita when she was overwhelmed or wanted to go out, and it was her weekend. He would do anything to be with his daughter all the time, so it never bothered him. But, now he is not around to be her crutch; he could tell this was getting to her now.

"It's been a few months now, the year will be done before you know it. I will be there in a few weeks as well, I hope that helps."

"Yeah, I know. Have a good show, good night."

Camryn disconnects the call before he can reply.

Jameson sits and breathes to himself. He loves routine and patterns, always has. It keeps him grounded and even-keeled. The more predictable his days are, the more productive he feels he will be.

Each day about three hours before the show, he takes an hour nap, gets up, and eats a bowl of cereal. Then he showers and changes into something comfortable and heads off to the show.

Today he has totally been out of his regular routine. No shower, no cereal, and definitely no peace.

Today's show will be interesting...

17

Showtime (Part 2)

braham is outside the window into the studio, counting down... three, two, pauses a beat, and points at Keisha.

"Welcome back everyone to the Dr. Black Love Experience, we have a short letter here but I think that most rather it be man or woman will be able to relate to," Keisha says into the microphone. She loves her new gig.

"Do we have any background on this letter at all Keisha?" asks Jameson.

"Single female, she does not give any information on her ethnicity but she is engaged, she and her fiancé have been together for four years, that's all she gives us."

"That's enough for now I guess... Please don't forget everyone the more information you give us, the more in-depth we can go. But it depends on what the subject matter is, perhaps any other details are irrelevant. Keisha please proceed."

"Dear Dr. Black Love, my fiancé and I have a good relationship, there isn't anything I can complain about enough normally to send you a letter. But I do have a bone to pick with him, and speaking to my girlfriends, it seems like a universal issue with men. Why do y'all trip when we say, we need to talk? Love, Miss Confused."

"Oh yeah, the age old question there...."

"That is a very good question if you think about it," exclaims Keisha.

"My response to this one is pretty simple," says Jameson.

"Nothing you say to our audience is simple, you'll take a two sentence question and turn it into a thirty minute dialogue."

"There are always layers to most of these questions but this one isn't too complex. First, I'll give some context to what I mean."

Jameson pauses as he often does before giving a response. He loves the banter between himself and Keisha; her energy has been magnetic for the show, she has a lovely spirit, and she is engaged every day. Today he truly appreciates her spirit and soulfulness.

"For most men, regardless of race, they have done some type of indiscriminate act to hurt their significant other. Two big parts of that sentence, I said most, not all, and regardless of race. We need to kill this terrible rumor that only men of color step out on their girlfriend or significant other, whatever you want to call the person you are dedicated to. Trust me, it don't matter what color they are, if someone is fine enough and they catch a man in the right or wrong mindset depending on which way you view it, it can go down. So, with that as a backdrop, a lot of men get caught. And when we do, we often hear those four frightening words... *we need to talk*."

"So it's all because of bad decision you made in the past, it requires you to have that stage fright so to speak and it just messes your species up?" Keisha pushes the envelope.

"Here you go with this species nonsense, why can't you just say men?"

They both laugh together.

"Cause you and the rest of your species aren't human, that's why damn it!" Keisha jokes.

"You're on one tonight, did your boyfriend piss you off before the show?" Jameson pushes back. Two can play this game.

"I told you a million times, I don't date boys and I do not have a significant other as you like to call it."

"Well maybe we need to find you a significant other so you can come in happy for once, hey Abraham, let's put that up on IG, who wants to date Keisha...." Jameson jokes.

"No, don't, I don't have time for that."

"We'll talk about that later, Abraham," Jameson says looking at Abraham, teasing his new co-host, "For those that don't know, Abraham is our engineer and knows not to pay any attention to Dr. Black Love and his nonsense."

Everyone laughs.

"OK, we'll get off of Keisha. And to answer your question, yes it does bring up bad memories. Like there is nothing good out of that conversation, so why wouldn't we react in a negative manner, even if it's something small? First thing we think is *what the hell did she see, find or go try to find?* See, you could be a good brotha, not doing anything and that will still make you think. And don't do that when we're at work, nothing else is getting done, we aren't any good after hearing that."

"Those are powerful words."

"They are, but you have to use them wisely as a woman. Don't do that and bring up something trivial or inconsequential," Jameson says.

"So are you telling Miss Confused to not say that to her fiancé?"

"If that's her tactic for trying to get attention or even play around with him, she should stop it. Not only are you engaging in unfair play, you may also alienate the person you love. If you have a good man, then support him and don't try to jam him up or have an 'I got you moment'. Men that are real men will take care of you, lift you up when needed, hold you when needed and love you when needed. Why mess that up with using that four-word sentence?"

"So, let's just say a female happens to find something and now she wants to talk about it, what should be her approach?" Keisha asks. This is intriguing to her.

"Before we even go there, why are you looking? And before you even answer, please don't give me that intuition B.S. all women claim to have. You know what that really means, I don't trust you and I will look until I find something to justify my trust issues. And when I do, it'll all be justified. And you know how I know most times it's your trust issue? Because on your quest to find something and you don't, do you ever go back and apologize for looking and not finding?"

Jameson pauses for five seconds, waiting for Keisha to say something.

"Hell no you don't, that's how you know it's not just him its you also. Seek and ye shall find, if you look and keep looking, and looking back six months, then a year, then two years you'll probably find something to get your win. But then what, you lose everything else. There are always three sides to every story, the two people involved each have a story and then there is the truth which is somewhere in the middle as the saying goes."

And before we get a million messages and emails I am not justifying whatever you found. I am saying to acknowledge your issues and also apologize if you don't find something, do that and let me know how that goes. He might tell your ass we need to talk then...."

Keisha and Jameson both laugh.

"Dr. Black Love, Abraham is telling us we are out of time for the night."

"Everyone have an amazing night and please remember, love only enters if the heart is willing, signing off, Dr. Black Love."

18

Pinkie Promise

R yann and Jameson are lying in bed. Ryann is asleep, but Jameson is still awake. His mind is racing; he slides out of bed, puts on some basketball shorts, and walks into the partially empty second bedroom.

The night has not surrendered to the daylight fully, so there is still some moonlight seeping through the partially open blinds into Zanita's room. Jameson turns and walks into the kitchen and takes a seat. He closes his eyes and gently moves his hands up and down over his eyes in a gentle up and down motion, making sure not to touch his face. Whenever he is stressed, this is his way of calming himself down.

Ryann gently walks out of the room, only wearing the blanket she was sleeping under, walks up behind him, hugs him, and whispers in his ear.

"Why are you awake Mr. Clarkson?"

"A few things on my mind, I didn't want to disturb you."

Ryann takes a seat across from him, wrapping herself under the blanket.

"Well talk to me, it's obviously not allowing you to sleep so get it off your chest."

Jameson hesitates... throughout his lifetime, he has rarely let people close to him. He may know a good amount of people and can walk around like a local celebrity in certain circles, but few know him, the real him. Outside of Eero and Kolby, few know more than bits and pieces of his life. He has purposely kept his circle small; it helps him maneuver the way he needs, keep secrets a secret, and avoid being hurt. He knows for a fact he can count on his two brothers; he's skeptical about the other 7+ billion people walking the earth.

Back when he and Ryann dated, he began to let her in. But when it ended, he decided that was too much for him to handle and left him way too fragile in the process. Since then, he has given most of himself to people he has been heavily involved with, most notably Camryn. She never knew all of him because he never allowed her to. That was all on him, so he carries that weight and guilt, but nobody knows but him.

Sometimes walking in the darkness alone, he feels is better for him, despite the people he may leave behind.

"Ryann, I just am starting to feel guilty about leaving Z. I miss her so much, she's the only thing in this world that loves me despite all the screwing up I've done, the missteps I make, she just loves me. That little girl has changed my world and I'm not there for her right now. I feel like a horrible father."

"I don't have any children but the seeds you planted with her are not going anywhere."

"Yeah but it's different being on FaceTime and actually being with someone, so they can feel your presence, so I can give her a hug, a kiss, tuck her into bed, comb her hair...."

Jameson gets up and walks over to the windows, and looks out at the moon.

"You're doing a fantastic job of staying in touch... Hell every time I call or text you, you're on the phone with her. She knows you love her," Ryann says reassuringly.

"It's not just her, it's me. I want to see her."

"Why don't you go see her then?"

"I can't leave the show for the first couple months, just need to get into a good groove."

"Then have her come here."

Jameson turns around.

"That's a good idea. I'll have her come for fall break. Thank you Ryann." He walks over and kisses her on the cheek.

"See sometimes talking to someone does help, you should try it more often."

"Easier said than done."

"What else is wrong with you?" asks Ryann.

This is what scared him about opening up; where do you draw the line and say enough is enough.

"Nothing..."

"Why are you so scared?"

"I don't know if you will love the real me, like when you get to the nooks and crannies, the ugly shit. I don't know if anyone really will. And even if you say you will, how do I know that you'll not see me differently or think less of me?" Jameson finds himself sharing more than he intended.

Ryann pauses before she answers; her relationship with Jameson has always been complicated. Before, she blamed him for all their issues, but as she matured, she realized that both she and Jameson had the same problem... they had trust issues.

"Jameson, I have loved you since we were teenagers. Nobody I have been with since has ultimately compared to you in my eyes. You get me, we can laugh, talk, relax, be dolled up or dressed down, we just click. To me that's so important, like I don't want to be the person I am at work because the man I am with doesn't fit me. With you I can just let my hair down and just be Ryann."

Jameson sits back down.

"Truthfully, you're the only person that I have ever let in. It was a long time ago but I gave everyone else the Heisman stiff arm... they never knew me totally. Camryn never knew the entire me, she saw a good portion but I never opened up to her."

"You married her."

"Yeah, I loved her but she didn't get the full experience of seeing the real me," Jameson admits.

"So what do we do?"

"I have no idea... I know that I want you to stay around and not go anywhere. I enjoy being with you, I look forward to seeing you, and I miss you when I don't see you."

"I feel the same way."

"I'm happy to hear that."

Ryann walks over to Jameson and straddles him.

"You have to promise me something."

"What's that?"

"That you won't run away from me like before. You have to start to trusting me and let me in. I don't want to be one of these six months of fun girls, I want us to really work on us. Can you promise me that?"

"I promise I will try."

"I don't like the word *try*, I want you to *do it* Jameson."

"How am I supposed to promise you it'll work?"

"I want you to promise me that you will put in the work to make it work and not punk out on me," Ryann says looking directly in his eyes.

"I can promise that."

Ryann holds up her pinkie finger.

"Pinkie promise me."

Jameson laughs.

"I'm serious, we taking it back to the old school."

Jameson obliges and pinkie promises.

"I want you to be happy."

"I am, just not totally, but that's not because of you Ryann, I promise you. Once I have Z here, I'll be different."

Ryann nods, "Well, buy her ticket so you can see your daughter."

"I will."

They kiss one another gently.

"I am going back to sleep."

Jameson nods, and Ryann goes back into the bedroom.

This is not the first promise Jameson has ever made, but he feels that Ryann is worth the effort. She saw him through his teenage years, and for no real fault of either, their relationship ended and grew into adulthood. He was happy they ran into one another and glad they could spend time with one another.

Now the hard part starts, actually letting her in without running away.

Where is Dr. Black Love when Jameson needs him, he thinks to himself.

19

Talk With Dad

Since he left, one of the voids in Jameson's life has not been seeing his father as often as he would like. Neither of them is phone people, so they don't call each other very often. When they do, the conversations are relatively short.

Thankfully, Mr. Clarkson has stepped into the 21st century and started texting over the last couple of years. That keeps the lines of communication open when speaking on the phone is difficult because of time zone differences or Jameson's hectic schedule.

Growing up, the two would listen to jazz on Saturday nights while Mrs. Clarkson attended church. It was kind of like their own peaceful time. Jameson would drink bottled root beer, and Mr. Clarkson would drink beer most times.

Sometimes they would speak about sports, women, the neighborhood while Mr. Clarkson was growing up, or current topics. No matter what, it was always a good time, and Jameson grew to look forward to those evenings. Even when his interest in other things began to grow as a teen and young adult, he would still sit with his dad for their Saturday conversations, as it came to be known.

Jamesons' father was an entrepreneur in the neighborhood for many years. He owned two corner stores, a barbershop, and the only gas station in the neighborhood. His father also ran a few numbers spots and some other shady-type businesses that he rarely talked about. He always owned a Cadillac, even still to this day and as previously mentioned, was always dapper.

With all that being true, Jameson most remembers his father as a great listener, loving him and his brother, and amazing at giving his perspective without making you feel pressured to do what he thought may be right. The latter being why Jameson was on his way to his old house now; it was Saturday early evening, so he knew his mother would be at church, and he needed to speak to his old man.

Jameson walks in and yells for his dad, who tells him to come downstairs and join him. As Jameson walks down the steps, he can hear *Bitches Brew* by Miles Davis, not one of his favorites but a classic nonetheless. It made him smile as he walked into his father's man cave.

"Dad, how you doing?" he says.

"I'm good, come have a seat but first get me another beer out of the fridge and one for yourself too."

"You know I don't drink beer much but for tonight, I think I'll do it."

Jameson gets the beers, opens them, and hands one to his father. They toast to old times and sit down.

Jameson's father looks at him and smiles.

"What's on your mind?"

"You know me too well... A few things to be honest. I miss Z a lot. I feel really guilty about not being there every day like I have been all of her life. It's starting to eat at me."

"You're a great dad, so don't beat yourself up too much. You sacrificed everything to stay out there, including a big part of yourself, period."

"But isn't that what a parent is supposed to do? I'm sure you and Mom sacrificed for us."

"Of course your situation is more extreme. We had family here, close friends, you had nothing out there. It's hard being alone, regardless of your reason why. And it's not like you moved just to do it, it was a better opportunity for you on all sides, professionally, socially, mentally."

"That's the truth, so how do I stop feeling guilty?" Jameson asks starting to feel a little better. His dad always knew the right words to say to speak peace and calm in his life. One day, he wants to be that for others, and for his own son some day.

"How do you feel now that you're back home?" his dad asks.

"I feel very good. I haven't been at peace for a long time."

"Zanita will be here in less than a year you told me. Then your world will be complete, so just realize this isn't a permanent move. Sometimes you have to sacrifice to come out on the better end of things."

Jameson nods in agreement, "Ryann thinks I should get her for fall break."

Mr. Clarkson's eyes get bigger, and he shakes his head in agreement.

"Ms. Ryann is back I see. She's a good girl, you should keep her around."

"She has trust issues, Dad."

"So do you, so do most of us. You know how you know you have a good woman?"

Jameson laughs to himself, "I used to but I don't think I do, tell me."

"When despite knowing all the dumb shit you've done, she is still willing to love you through it. You left Ryann for no good reason and here you are ten years later and she's still around, she's a keeper," his dad says bluntly.

"I know, and this sounds bad but I don't think I'll ever do better than her."

"Yeah that does sound bad, don't say that around her."

They both laugh.

"What I mean is, if I had to come up with a perfect woman, she would be it. Nobody is perfect but someone that accepts me for me, supports me in the way I need, she does all of that and always has."

"What do you do for her?"

"I think she trusts me, which is very hard for her. And she knows that I will do everything I can to make her happy."

"Just don't do anything stupid, you got that in your genes. Most things I passed to you are good so sorry," his dad jokes.

Jameson smiles and takes a long drink of his beer.

"You should come on the show one day."

"I don't think those young people want to hear from an old man," his dad waves his hand, brushing off the idea.

"They would love it, you're my father so everyone would want to know where I get it from."

"Well I could come down there and spit some knowledge."

"I'm going to make that happen, we could do it every week or something," Jameson starts to toy around with the idea.

They tap beer bottles to the proposal.

"How are things with the show off the air?"

"Things are very good, we have good chemistry and it's clicking much better and faster than I thought it would to be honest. Keisha and Abraham are definite pluses to the show, and it's been a seamless transition."

"It seems like it, and I think the show is better with Keisha. It's always good to have a different voice on a show like yours."

They continue to talk about random things from sports to politics to re-living childhood memories for Jameson.

This is one of those nights that reminds Jameson of why he moved back home. One never knows how much longer you could have with a loved one. Being home allows him to do nothing but talk with his father and still be completely happy about it.

No need for any frills, just some cold beer, good music, cigars, and laughs. A perfect night.

"The standard is the standard."

- Head Coach Mike Tomlin

20

Showtime (Part 3)

"We have the last letter of the night Dr. Black Love," explains Keisha. "And we're going to get into a hot button topic, one that will definitely create debate and discussions but this what we do here."

"Please proceed Keisha," says Jameson.

The new format of the show is still not 100% settled with Jameson. When he ran the show himself, he could pick and choose which topics to discuss, strategically place them at certain points of the show, hold letters back, or not even discuss topics that he wasn't comfortable touching. Now, with the show simulcasted live online, they want to get an honest look into how it is and, more importantly, how he reacts. He cannot hide behind the veil of Dr. Black Love as an anonymous to many faces any longer; he is out there for the masses to consume.

His struggle with change has been a constant all of his life. However, he can put up a good front as he has mastered from his childhood and feels he has a doctorate in putting up a good front in situations where you may not be totally comfortable. Growing up in neighborhoods where you can quickly be challenged at any time makes you develop this outer shell of toughness, even if your insides are paranoid about the situation.

With Keisha having control over what questions he answers, he has no way of knowing what will be thrown his way. But, unfortunately, vulnerability is not an easy foe to fight for him. Typically, violence has been the easiest weapon of choice in the fight in his past.

"Dear Dr. Black Love, I am in quite a predicament now. I have been dating my boyfriend for almost two years now. Our relationship has been very good, I have very few complaints outside of trivial things. We get along well, our families both like each other, things have been very good. At least until about two months ago, we had a very big circumstance happen.

I found out I was pregnant. Now we are good financially, we're both professionals, we are in our late 20's, so it's not like we're kids. The problem is I don't feel it's the right time to bring a life into this world and he wants nothing more than to have a family. And I feel guilty about the way I feel now, but it's not the right time for me. What do you think? Signed, Miss Not the Right Time."

Keisha stops and looks at Jameson.

Jameson has his eyes closed, rubbing his forehead slowly. Then, he looks up at the ceiling and breathes out slowly.

"Dr. Black Love, are you good?" Keisha asks.

"Yes, I'm fine."

"There are two issues that Miss Not the Right Time is dealing with," Jameson starts in, "Let's tackle the easier of the two and one we have discussed a number of times in the past. When we get into relationships, we need to discuss things that are of real importance. We tend to focus on small, immaterial things that in the long run will have little impact on our new relationship, especially in the beginning.

We put on the front of a good person, eventually that wears off and we get to meet the real person in front of us. But from there we rarely discuss big issues, and the one that we usually neglect is how we feel about *what-if* situations. Like what if one of my parents gets sick and we live together, would you be comfortable with them living with us?... or what if the person I have a child with is in need financially, would you have a problem with me helping them?... or in this situation if we become pregnant, what would you want us to do with the child?

So our first lesson is at some point before we get in too deep, have some of these discussions so you can know what the other person is feeling. Clearly they did not do that in this relationship. And some things have a tendency to bite you at the wrong time, as she mentioned career wise, this is a not a good time for her."

"That's a very good point, why don't we do that?" Keisha asks to keep the conversation moving.

"We react to things as opposed to be proactive, we like to stay in our bubble when we are falling in love and don't want to rock the boat with tougher issues or questions. It's much easier to push these discussions off than it is to go to dinner at night and just talk about our day with our significant other," Jameson continues. "Now, getting on to the next subject, this is much trickier and deeper. And it brings up a much broader topic in society like you mentioned, Keisha... abortion, or as I like to call it, the struggle over power."

"So abortion is not about the baby, it's about the power over the baby?" asks Keisha, now she's sitting up in her seat. This is getting into a touchy subject.

"It's about men wanting to control women and have the power over what they can do with their bodies. 99% of the time if it doesn't have anything to do with sex or something sexual, men could give a damn about a woman's body or anything that happens to it. But when it comes to a baby or the right to chose to have a baby, then they get all up in arms."

Keisha interjects, "But what about women that are anti abortion, they have the same body parts that other women do. What do you think about that?"

"It's still power, it's who has the authority to say what you will do and not do. Certain people in this world love that influence. Abortion is about me saying you can do this and not that.

Now here is the kicker, since we're on the subject. It's mainly white men in power causing all the ruckus. You will get a lot of these people that bring in Biblical or religious references to support their argument. Let's point out how that's hypocritical...

Those same people who are so up in arms about a women having the ability to chose what to do are the same people who will turn their back on most children born into poverty or lesser situations. They could give a damn about a poor kid, but they will fight tooth and nail about their mother not being able to get an abortion, you're born a few months later and they'll turn and walk away from helping that same child in a destitute situation.

So theoretically they are contributing to more crime, more violence, and the cycle of poverty. If they really read the same Bible they claim to know so well that isn't a principle of God either. If you love people you don't take options away from them, then provide them no help on the other side. That's not Godly in my book, that's cruel and hateful."

Abraham looks at Jameson with wide eyes and puts both hands in the air as if to say what happened.

"I have my engineer looking really shook right now. It's the truth, and anyone that says otherwise is trying to pull one over on you, simple as that."

"Dr. Black Love has spoken people, let us know what you have to say please. Hit us up on IG, Facebook, the website, holla at us. Any last words?" Keisha interrupts and pushes to close the show before it gets even more tense. *Clearly Dr. Black Love hit a wall. What's got his panties in a bunch tonight?*

"As always, remember... love only enters your heart if it is willing to receive it, signing off one last time, Dr. Black Love."

Abraham immediately walks into the studio.

"Jameson, what the hell was that?"

"Don't try to come in here and lecture me, I didn't say anything inflammatory or derogative. It was all the truth."

"That doesn't matter, it's about the people cutting our checks, if they have a problem with it, then it's a problem."

"We have the highest rated show in our time slot, we're about to be syndicated. What the hell they gonna do to us?" Jameson says unbothered.

"Keisha can you help me out here?" Abraham looks at Keisha for support.

"Nope, not really."

Abraham slams himself into a seat.

"I promise you Justin will speak to you tomorrow."

"So be it if that's the case," Abraham gives in, sighs and shakes his head.

Jameson grabs his backpack and walks out of the studio.

21

Principal's Office

As Abraham had predicted, Justin called Jameson into an 8 a.m. meeting in his office downtown the following day. Jameson was annoyed that the meeting was so early, but Justin's office was also in the penthouse of the building; their offices were many floors below.

Jameson did not believe one could lead people if they weren't close to them. How could he feel the pulse of the staff if he was never close to them?

The disdain for Justin grew as he glanced throughout his office, pictures with celebrities, golf outings, dinners spread in multiple locations. His desk was in disarray with excel spreadsheets, rating sheets, and other papers randomly thrown around on his desk. He had no personal photos, no family pictures, and it looked as if he had never unpacked anything outside of his celebrity pictures in a blatant attempt, in Jameson's mind, to gloat.

Jameson glanced outside the floor-to-ceiling walls into the distance. Downtown Pittsburgh is a stone's throw from the old neighborhood. Rarely as a child would he and his family venture downtown; it was like a foreign territory. Banks, businesses, and town hall were all down there, yet it felt many miles away. Most times, when someone on his block was downtown, it wasn't for anything good. They were either being booked for jail or working some menial job they hated and cursed as they took public transportation for their shift.

As he grew up, his father would take them downtown to experience something different from their neighborhood. They would see lawyers, judges, business people walking around eagerly and quickly. At times they would get strange looks, and it would make them feel out of place.

Jameson always remembered two things his father always told him: always look a man in the face when speaking and never move out of the way for someone walking down the street. The former is something that Jameson learned in the neighborhood; if you looked down when speaking, it meant you were either lying or unsure of yourself—neither of which would lead to any positive outcomes.

The latter Jameson never entirely understood until he was older. His father would always warn him about not being subservient to anyone; regardless of their race or stature, they were either a man or woman and no better than them. If he or his brother moved when walking down the street, their father would grab them and make them walk straight.

"If they don't move for you, you don't move either," his dad would say.

Jameson could remember they would bump into someone several times, and their father never said excuse me unless they did. "Don't let them disrespect you, if they do it once, you'll never earn it back," is another quote their father would echo to them repeatedly.

Now, as Jameson glanced out far over the neighborhood he grew up in, he wasn't about to let Justin bump into him without getting bumped right back.

Justin opens the door and quickly walks to his desk, and sits. Jameson could tell he was a bit tense, so he opened up with the small talk, something he hated, but he would play the game.

"How you doing Justin?" Jameson asks.

Justin sighs, "To be honest I'm a little stressed...."

Jameson stands up, walks over to a few pictures, and cuts him off before he continues.

"I noticed you don't have any family photos, just outings and things like that. Where's your wife and kids?"

Justin is a bit thrown off.

"I really haven't had time to… to, put up anything. I got here a couple weeks before you did. So I don't really spend much time in here," he manages to say as he watches the new guy prance around his office, snooping and making him uncomfortable a bit.

"Move your office then, I'm sure this view cuts into the budget," Jameson points at the stadiums, the clouds as if to be impressed.

"I know what you're thinking but this wasn't my choice to be up here. This office was here well before I started, they used it to entice us to set up in the building a couple years ago. I prefer to be around the studios, around the real energy."

"Having options is always nice," Jameson says as he sits down. "What's the problem Justin?"

Justin clears his throat, "Well, the executives didn't really like the end of the show last night to be honest. It's kind of a touchy subject with everything that's going on in this country, and it's not really the subject matter of the show, at least in their opinion."

Jameson nods his head in silence and stares back at Justin but says nothing.

Justin grows even more uncomfortable with the silence and speaks again, "The show is doing great, I think even better than what I thought at this point. So, there isn't anything to discuss with that part."

"What's your opinion, Justin?"

"About what exactly?" Justin asks cautiously. He hates these types of conversations. Not the best part of his job, nonetheless, it is part of the job.

"About the show last night, what do you personally think?" Jameson asks Justin sincerely.

"I have two thoughts about it... First, you're absolutely correct. Nothing you said wasn't true. And quite frankly I don't care who it makes uncomfortable; and if it makes someone feel some type of way, then they probably need to search deeper for a reason why."

"And your second thought?" Jameson knows there's a big BUT in there somewhere.

"Neither one of us writes our own checks. So from time to time, everyone has to do shit we don't like."

"Like most places we have freedom until we piss off the rich people, then we have to be checked... Am I being fired?"

"Hell no, they just want you to apologize," Justin says.

Jameson laughs out loud at the suggestion.

"That's not gonna happen. I'm not apologizing for something I firmly believe in and that isn't wrong. That's my integrity, that's who I am. So you can tell whoever is sending the message to kiss my ass."

Justin nods in agreement.

"I actually figured you would say that. And I wouldn't do it either. So I told them we wouldn't be doing that."

"What did they say to that?"

Justin looks at his phone.

"Nothing, I haven't heard back from them since."

"Is that why you're nervous?"

Justin stands up and walks to the windows.

"Yes. I don't like the silence, that's not good."

"So we just wait?" Jameson asks.

"Yeah that's why I called you, so you could wait with me."

They both laugh.

"You're not so bad Justin, I didn't know what to think about you when we first met."

"I get that a lot, I wear suits and have to act a certain way but I'm no different that you Jameson," Justin relaxes a little.

Jameson looks side-eyed at him.

"Let me explain... I started in this business making like $10 a hour, the assistant to the assistant to the interns assistant. I've done every job in radio media, so I got here because I put in the work, and I know what I'm doing. I didn't get anything handed to me. And I know you are and will be huge in this space, but we need to always be cognitive of our audience and our bosses. The bigger you get, the harder that is to manage."

"I know what you mean, but the bigger we get the less they can do to us. We'll be fine." Jameson is unbothered by the bosses. He didn't come all this way to bend now.

"I hope so," Justin turns and looks out the window again.

Twenty minutes pass and both men's phones go off at the same time.

Jameson reads the message.

"It's a press release from corporate. They apologized for last night's rant by yours truly, they are suspending the show indefinitely, and that's it."

Justin shrugs his shoulders and sits down at his desk.

Jameson sits down as well.

Justin goes into his desk and pulls out two shot glasses, some Bourbon, and pours two double shots.

"Let's do a toast," says Justin.

"A toast to what? I just got suspended indefinitely."

"You don't get it, You're too big to fire bro, congratulations."

Justin holds up his glass, Jameson grabs his; they tap glasses and take a drink.

"When will they bring us back?" Jameson asks, a little nervous but following the lead of his new business companion.

"When the public demands it. And I think your fans will be all over this, don't sweat it at all," Justin is quite sure. He's seen it too many times when corporate try to rid the world of a star before the world is ready to be rid of him or her.

Jameson isn't sold on the news.

"I wouldn't lie to you Jameson, you and the show will be fine."

"Alright, I'm gonna go, I'll check you later." Jameson heads out and closes the door behind him.

22

The Point

*J*ameson walks outside of the building and stands for a moment. On the one hand, he was pleased they didn't cancel the show outright, but on the other, he did not like being censored.

His goal was always to be independent, and he was, but with his new contract and station, he had people above him that he probably would never meet that ultimately called the shots. He felt hopeless; now, would any controversial topic end with the same result? It was nice to know he was big enough not to be fired, but having the preverbal thumb on his neck was not something he had fully considered the full gravity it would have on his career and his voice.

As Jameson stood in the corridor of the building, looking out, people walking back and forth. That feeling of not knowing where he would go reminded him of when he walked downtown with his Father as a child. He felt lost and hopeless, he was not in control, and that feeling is something he always attempted to avoid rather it be in his career, relationships, or friendships. Living in ambiguity and confusion leaves him in a very negative space, and he works very hard to quell those feelings as quickly as possible.

Unfortunately, he was not in total control as he was back west, and he would have to wait for this one out. With bigger money comes bigger responsibility, so finding some balance between Dr. Black Love and Jameson would have to happen. He could not afford to be reckless; too much was riding on him to succeed in his new situation. He moved his entire life back home, so failing was not an option or consideration.

As a teenager and into his younger adulthood, when times would get a bit much for Jameson, he would walk down to the Point. The Point is a landmark where all three rivers meet, a fountain typically only on during warmer months. And most importantly, for Jameson, there was solitude. There are benches spaced out and the peace of the river—a perfect place for his current mindset. He placed his air pods in his ears, turned on John Coltrane's *Blue Train*, and he started on his way by foot.

Jameson notices the difference in how the city was from his younger days. More laid-back outfits replaced the stuffy suits, and he feels a happier tone while walking down the streets. He is delighted to see the change; progress in a city with deep roots in being separated is a step in the right direction. He stops inside a drug store, since he can't find a Mom-n-Pop store, to grab something to drink and continue on his way.

Jameson passes the Wyndham hotel and walks onto Fort Pitt and to the fountain. He notices the families on picnics, children running around, and those taking in the sun. He finds one of the benches alongside the three rivers heritage trail and sits down.

Jameson did not notice the plethora of text messages and notifications he received while on his excursion to his destination. In the new age of social media, it only takes a tiny spark to create a whirlwind of news. The show has a significant following on social media, that's how Jameson built the brand, and they are out in full force in support of what was said and against his indefinite suspension.

Jameson does not respond to anything and just sit in silence and awe. It is a beautiful day, mid 70's, mild humidity, and partly sunny. Boats sailing up and down all three rivers, and as much as things has changed, this is very much the same as he remembered from many years ago. It is just as calm as he remembered; it is perfect for the moment.

Jameson's phone vibrates. It's the love of his life.

> Hey babe, call me when you get a moment 💋

Ryann

Jameson calls.

"Hey, sorry I'm just detaching from all the madness."

"I figured but at some point you need to at least respond to a message or something," Ryann says, relieved that she hears his voice now. Crisis diverted.

"I don't know what to say to anyone. I can't change the decision, I can't do shit which I hate," Jameson admits, still feeling hopeless but trying to stay strong.

"Well I think your followers are making enough noise that shows their love and support of what you've built. You should check it out, and I think you need to let them know you appreciate what they're doing."

"I will, I need to make sure my mind is clear. I want to make the right statement at the right time, kind of a big moment."

"It is, that's because you're kind of a big deal now," Ryann says teasingly, but realizing her man kind of is a big deal.

"Nah, apparently I'm just an employee that can be shut down if I say something about old white men, who apparently call the shots where I work," Jameson spurts out.

"I think you're way more powerful than they realize, and they're going to see it. It's already started, once you tap back into what's going on you'll see. So it seems like you're good... you don't seem upset or disappointed."

"I'm pissed but it's more controlled. I don't think it has anything to do with Justin, we actually had a pretty good conversation about it and we both found out at the exact same time through an email. I may have been a little hard on him when I met him."

"Possibly but at least you gave him a chance to redeem himself. Where are you?" Ryann asks.

"Oh, one of my favorite places here, down here at the Point."

"It stinks down there...."

"If you pay attention to it, yes it does. But I always came down here when we would have a fight or something would be going on that I needed to get away. It's kind of like its own world, it's always been peaceful to me."

"OK, enjoy yourself, some of us have to work to get paid."

"Here you go, I work hard too."

"I know you do, baby, I'll see you later."

"OK, good bye."

Jameson continued to ignore the vibrations from his phone and notifications. Instead, he sipped on his soda, ate his potato chips, and just enjoyed the breeze. He figures he can hold out for a bit before letting all the stress of the day get to him.

23

Stressed Out

Kolby is in a meeting with Paul Romano. He is sitting back on a couch in Paul's downtown office. Dressed up for the occasion wearing a black button-down shirt with slacks, black gator slip-ons, Kolby is still uncomfortable, uneasy, and tired.

"So what you're telling me, Paul, is there is no way to make this go away?" Kolby asks.

Paul walks over to Kolby and hands him a drink, and sits next to him.

"My friend, these cases only go away when you cut a check. Otherwise it'll drag on, you'll pay more money in lawyer fees and probably end up paying for their lawyer fees, too. You pay more in damage to your reputation, making you drink more and grow more aggravated than anything else."

Kolby ignores the drinking comment and finishes his drink.

"I feel like paying someone off is admitting guilt, and I'm not guilty. I might be guilty of being stupid to involve myself with someone I employ but nothing else is accurate."

"If this was kindergarten, Kolby, then you'd be correct. Think about it, you're going into court, civil court I remind you, being the rich black guy that took advantage of the poor black girl. In civil court, that normally doesn't end well."

"I don't like it."

Paul slaps Kolby on the knee.

"Kolby, I've been involved with you for many years. You care about your money and your reputation more than anything. The time is for clear thinking, not going out in a blaze of glory right now. This isn't about money for me, it's about you coming out on the other end being able to function as you did going in. Think big picture and long game here."

"So, if I decide to pay, do I admit being guilty."

"No, not at all."

"Think of all these celebrities and athletes that settle civil cases, they aren't admitting their guilty. It's a payoff, better for both parties. Few people want to appear in court and spill what's happened to them to the public. It's a very respectful thing to do."

"But what about the next former employee that I fire, and the next one after that. This could be the start of a shit load of cases," Kolby says, feeling a little backed up against the wall.

"You can't control what may happen, but this case will and is happening now. Let's worry about the present, tomorrow we'll deal with at that point."

Kolby thinks for a moment.

"Life isn't fair. I started out in a single parent home. I built everything I have with my own bare hands. No rule book was given to me, I had to learn with every victory and defeat. Seems like no matter what this country never lets a black man go unscathed."

"What do you mean?"

"We can only operate in certain lanes, and even within those lanes only attain certain heights. Perfect example, what if I wanted to be a black Hue Hefner, Paul? You think that shit would have ever happened?"

"I really don't know."

Kolby shakes his head at Paul.

"You know the answer to that is no. I'd be called a black pimp running hoes. But for the old white guy, it's seen as art and a great business plan ran by a great business mind."

"He had some run-ins with the law."

"Comes with the territory but it's a lot different than it would be for someone that looks like me, that's my point, Paul. The shit ain't fair, never has been."

"You're right but what can we do to change it?" Paul asks, shrugging his shoulders.

"I wish I knew."

"Your friend seems to be able to change it a little bit at least."

"What friend?"

"The one with the radio show."

"Jameson?" Kolby asks surprisingly. *Man, please.*

"Yeah he got suspended for some comments he made last night. I heard about it on the news."

"I don't watch the news," Kolby dismisses the comment.

"You should, it'll keep you informed. My point is he has a strong social media following, that's been the great equalizer in the last few years."

"I don't fool with that shit. I have some people do social media for me. I don't get involved myself personally."

"That's where real change is happening, it gives everyone a voice. Which can be both good and bad, but at least it gives people a chance to express themselves."

"I get it, I get it, Paul."

Kolby stands up and shakes Paul's hand.

"Let's work on getting the deal done, and hope this isn't a trend."

"I'll get working on it."

As Kolby walks out of the office, he comes to the conclusion that Paul will never really understand his plight. However, he does appreciate the relationship Paul and himself have built over the years.

Kolby will leave, and around midnight be dealing with a drunk server, a bartender making watered down drinks, and have almost to break up a fight. Paul will bill him for this meeting, have three other meetings doing the same thing, drive home to his multi-million dollar neighborhood, fall asleep around 10 p.m., and repeat the same thing tomorrow.

They do business together, but they come from different worlds.

24

Getting Dirty

Eero is in his downtown office going over the campaign numbers by himself, and the television is on in the background.

"There it is again," he says to himself.

The campaign is based primarily upon the merits of the candidates. They both are qualified for the position. Eero has been in the position for some time and has done an excellent job. He has an impeccable reputation and has made sure the city is in a good place from a financial standpoint, given the constraints he has to deal with sometimes.

Unfortunately, the recent ads from the other side are now putting things into a space that he does not want to go. The ads are doing the classic, taking one-liners and making them fit into a misrepresented agenda. It's an old-school tactic, but considering the current political climate and how many potential voters gather their varying viewpoints, it can work, as has been proven at higher levels of elected officials.

Eero is going over recent numbers conducted on the race. He is still up according to the numbers, but to this point, it's been child's play, now the heat is going to start turning up with only six weeks until voting.

The City Controller position is not as sexy as the Mayor or even as well known as a City Councilperson, but extremely important nonetheless. You don't typically get many chances to speak publicly in front of the voters; there isn't much of a rush to see someone responsible for counting the beans of the city. So, these ads are important to Eero. Although he has kept it above the board throughout his time in this position, he feels that it's important to show integrity in his ads. After all, if you lie in one area of life, why wouldn't you be inclined to do so in another? And if that's your character, how can someone be trusted with the city's budget at their discretion?

Edward "Ed" Paul, Eero's campaign manager, walks into the office.

"Hey Eero, how's it going?" asks Ed as he takes a seat.

Ed was a veteran of local politics, a tremendous asset to Eero in his career. He has helped several other politicians in the city's history. Eero has always felt that he helped him cross over and guided him in appealing to other ethnicities in the city, especially the white population that dominates the percentages. "Without their vote, you have no shot," Ed told him when he first put his team together. He followed what he told him about being presented as a family man, great integrity, and track record to keep it above the bar, and he would win, and it's worked each time to this point.

Eero turns off the television and looks at Ed for a few seconds.

"I don't know, I don't feel good about these ads that have come up over the last day or so."

"Yeah, I've seen them. He's using your past business partner's track record on one of them, and using your other business interests against you in another."

"Right, you don't see a problem with that?"

"Outside of it being total bullshit, no I don't. What else can he do, he has to try something in order to drum up some kind of doubt. He can't attack you on merit, so this is the road he's chosen," Ed says matter of factly.

"Mr. Campaign Manager, how do we proceed?"

"We have two roads we can take. We can fight back with the same tactics, using real evidence or we can ignore it."

"What do you think we should do?" Eero knows what he's going to say.

"Normally I would say ignore it, but I don't feel that we can. I think he wants to win and he'll do whatever it takes to win."

Eero was in politics, but not into it. He left the private sector because he felt he had an obligation to give back. He lost money moving into this position; he does not get stock options, bonuses, or even much of a pat on the back.

Every four years, you have to raise money to run for office and do the same thing on repeat until you either retire or lose. Eero's demeanor of being quiet can sometimes be mistaken as being passive. He preferred to use his mind over his fists, even when growing up around a bunch of fighters. When necessary, he would turn to hand-to-hand combat, but he preferred to outthink everyone.

"You know Mary said it would come down to this, I hate when she's right."

Ed chuckles.

"All men hate when their wife is right but they normally are. We just like to take credit for it."

"Her father said he would help pull some strings but I don't want his help, I'm trying to move us away from being under his thumb."

"You should have thought of that before you married her. A family like that always sticks together."

"I agree..."

"About the campaign or your wife?"

"Hell, both!"

They both laugh.

"Let's do what we need to do to win, being passive or looking like we're hiding is not the route to take."

Ed nods in agreement.

Eero's phone vibrates, and he picks it up. A group text with him and the fellas.

Kolby: Come down to the spot 2nite

Jameson: After 2day, I can damn sure use some adult beverages

Eero: Shit, me too. See you both

"Let's get to work," says Eero to his team. Eero picks up his phone again, "Siri, text my wife..." He types...

Eero: Tell your Father I need him.

Mary: I already did

Eero puts his phone down. "Looks like things have already started."

25

Grand Experiment

Kolby's lounge has been around for some time in the city. It's the type of place that lets you know how small of a town Pittsburgh can be.

You can run into someone you have not seen since high school one night, and they can sometimes seem the same way as they were in high school. Same neighborhood, dressing the same way, and even thinking the same way, unfortunately.

But, on the other side, there is some appreciation for the fact that people will show you love and respect for what you have accomplished. It can be an odd paradox to find yourself in, you feel bad on the one hand, but you still show them love on the other.

Kolby has constantly struggled to push the envelope with his lounge; he attempts to mix crowds of young professionals that moved into the city during the technology boom over the past five to ten years, along with the locals, as described earlier. His menu reflects the same range, from cheap local beer to expensive champagne. It's a delicate balancing act that he has done well with, but has to keep tabs on to keep the balance going strong continuously.

Most evenings, Kolby is front and center, sitting in the corner of the bar in his favorite seat. It gives him the ability to see the lounge from all sides; he is not a hands-off owner by any stretch of the imagination. He oversees the bar, checks the kitchen; he will seat you if the hostess is taking too long for his liking. His name is on the building literally, and despite the success of his other businesses, this lounge is probably the most important to him.

He is the keeper of the city's black culture; the other places have come and gone, but he is still alive and kicking. He takes pride in it and does not take his stature for granted.

Tonight though is not one of the nights where he cares about that. Kolby and Eero are in the office as Jameson steps into the room.

"Well look here Eero, we are blessed with the presence of Dr. Black Love," Kolby teases.

"Shit, he's on suspension... indefinitely apparently," Eero chimes in.

Jameson gives dap to Eero and then to Kolby.

"Pour me a shot of tequila bruh," Jameson says to Kolby.

"You're doing shots? Shit tonight is about to get real!" Kolby says as he pours a shot and hands it to Jameson.

"Let me tell you something, I have never been suspended, expelled or anything in my entire life until today. And it was for telling the truth. You know we tell our children and you hear growing up to be honest, the good guy wins, hard work will always pay off...," Jameson drinks the entire shot, "all that shit is a fucking lie."

Jameson holds up the shot glass and tosses it to Kolby.

"Give me a double."

"So what happened, nothing you said wasn't true," Eero says in defense of Jameson.

"I basically offended some old white men that you can't in my situation. Unless you're like Kolby, you always have someone to answer to."

"I'll stop you right there, shit I had to agree today to start settlement talks. Paul says it's the best route to take, less expensive and less complicated," Kolby says defeatedly.

"Damn, how much will that cost you?" asks Jameson.

"I didn't even ask, I know it won't be cheap but going to court, having to testify, fighting with a server who can claim victim, and then cutting a check after all that ain't worth it. So I agreed, what the hell else can I do?" Kolby shrugs his shoulders.

"Pay now or it'll cost you more later basically," says Jameson.

All three say in unison, "Basically."

Kolby finishes his drink and nods in agreement.

"I'll add to the fucked up day news," exclaims Eero. "Today I had to agree to let my father-in-law use his tactics on the campaign, my wife already asked him anyway. I don't want to be like a politician, and I hate having her father all in our shit. It's like I can never break away from her family."

Jameson looks over at Eero.

"Eero, I gotta tell you something. The other day Mary stopped over, unannounced of course," Jameson fills his friend in. So much has happened, he totally forgot about his conversation with Mary. Until now.

"For what?" asks Eero.

"It was about the election, she said you wasn't listening to her about what needed to be done."

"She was right about that one. But, I can admit when I'm wrong...."

"But there's more... She's just not happy with her role bruh. Like I think she wants to do more than be a house wife, playing in the back from what she said."

"That's what we agreed to. You can't change the rules in the middle of the game," Eero says, starting to get a little agitated. She can tell this dude she's unhappy and don't part her lips in front of him.

"That's women for you, they want shit and then when you give it to them, they change their minds. That's exactly why I will never get married," interjects Kolby.

"Technically you aren't married but you are, to money."

"Fuck outta here Jameson."

"No seriously, we're all grown men and friends in here. Think about it, outside of us two, who have you always been loyal to, fought hard to keep and protected, your money. So that's your wife, and part of the reason you're so pissed about having to write a check," Jameson blurts out.

"I know you think you're some philosopher because of your show but between us, you still the same negro that wore some high waters the first day of high school," Kolby says.

Eero and Kolby burst out laughing.

"Whatever, I'm just telling you both the truth. Don't have shit to do with a show or anything. I'm just a smart ass person, with knowledge, son."

"Tell that shit to someone on your show, we ain't buying it," says Eero.

Eero and Kolby both give each other some dap.

"Seriously though, Eero for her to come speak to me, I'm concerned," Jameson gets serious for a minute.

"Me too, I just don't know what to do. I'm in the middle of a campaign, I still have my job to do, I'm the only one bringing a check home at the moment. Who has the time for this on top of all that right now?" Eero exclaims.

"You gotta make time, hell I'll watch the kids or something one night. Go to the casino, well shit you can't really gamble I guess... Just do something together by yourselves. I don't want to see you two not together, not you two."

"I can help too...." Kolby says.

"Nah, Kolby, we don't need your help on this one. You aren't exactly the subtle or sensitive type. And Mary, well don't like you all like that," Jameson says jokingly.

"Everybody loves Mr. Kolby, the girls y'all have you only have because I let you have 'em."

"Speaking of that, what's up with Ryann Mr. Clarkson?" asks Eero.

Jameson smiles and chuckles to himself.

"I knew that would come up. Things are good."

"That's it, things are good."

"My wife can come talk to you about our marriage and you can't give us nothing more than *things are good* with the love of your life. Come on with that shit," Eero says.

"You know I don't talk about myself very much."

"Might as well start today, I think we all need some new direction considering what's going on with us collectively," says Eero.

"OK, fine. Ryann and I have been kicking it hard since I came back home. Not every night but I speak to her daily, we check-in with each other, she kind of knows where I am most of the time...."

Eero interjects, "Wow, that's big for you. You're the one that is incognito to basically any woman, and your six-month-rule, I'm sure went over well with her."

"Yeah, that didn't go over well at all!" Jameson says.

They all laugh.

Jameson continues, "But I told her where I was with things. I don't even know how to be serious with someone anymore, I lost the urge to go deep with someone, ever since my divorce I've just been focused on Z and my career. There's always women around but they have been non-factors, I have not even given them a chance."

"But this ain't any woman, this is Ryann. You loved her since we was teenagers. She popped your cherry and you ain't been the same since," says Kolby.

"Don't ever tell her that shit, she'll never let me live it down... But, I don't know, things are good, we'll see what happens."

"All jokes aside, I hope things work out for you with her, she's a keeper," says Kolby, holding up his glass to him.

Jameson nods in appreciation.

"What about the station, any word on what's going to happen?" asks Eero.

"Nope, nothing."

"So they just suspended you and that's it, no talk internally about how long, nothing at all?" asks Kolby.

"No, I know as much as you all do. Small press statement, we got it at the same time as everyone else."

"Fans are giving it to the station though, your shit has been trending all day. That's big, if that keeps up you'll be fine," Eero says. He knows all too well the power of social media and public cry.

"When I was talking to Paul about settling, we had a small conversation about life not being fair for us as black men. I didn't get into a deep discussion with him because he won't ever really get it. But if you think about it, we're basically rats in a huge 400+ year experiment. From slavery which is still the state our people have been in longer than any other in this country, to how the police were first formed to hunt slaves, to Jim Crow laws, to zoning laws, to COINTELPRO, to assassinating our leaders, and now even, we're just lab rats hoping to get that small piece of cheese.

A lot of us get caught in traps, and never even get a crumb, occasionally we get a big crumb, but then they continue to work on bringing us down. Look at Bill Cosby, he was 80 something years old rotting in jail for some shit from the 70's. And what's the real reason, his ass was getting too powerful, they not about to let some black man own NBC, hell no.

Today, I just felt like it don't matter what I do, I'll never be able to have the same life as Paul, and that shit pisses me off. Not that I want his same life, it's just the fact that no matter how hard I work, no matter how smart I am, I have damn near a zero percent chance at the same lifestyle he has. And the worst part is that we both know it and can't do anything about it," Kolby spits nothing but truth to his best friends.

All three sit in silence. Kolby had just dropped a nuclear bomb into the conversation. In these small tribunal conversations, truth is distorted or left out totally, often leading to discussions on sports or gossip. Communion like this only comes from years of trust and love. Opening up your true feelings to anyone that does not care about you leaves you vulnerable, and that was too great a risk for any of them to participate in.

"That's some real shit right there, Kolby. Makes you think what's the point?" asks Eero.

"All that's true, but just as much as those powers are against us, look what we've done despite it. Kolby, you are the epitome of what we should be as black men, strong, independent, not giving a fuck and you bust your ass every day to prove yourself over and over.

Eero, you are a fucking genius with numbers, you have a beautiful family, you built and sold a financial institution and took a job for the City because you wanted to. You two are my heroes bruh, without question," Jamesons says, maybe feeling the shots a bit. He's a little... a LOT emotional and this is a safe space for him to be.

"Let's not sell yourself short, Jameson. We all need these flowers today. You have reinvented yourself a number of times, you have been knocked on your ass, got up, flipped the script and built a character out of your own failures to build a brand, flip the script and get a company to pay you to come back home and monetize that shit. That's genius also, it isn't perfect, which I know you wanted, but it's your story and it's beautifully imperfect," Eero says to lift up his friend.

All three hold up their drinks and toast each other.

They continue to talk and speak throughout the night; many years ago, this was their standard Friday evening. Eat, drink and laugh, figure out the answers to the world and see how things went the following Friday night. These are the nights that Jameson moved back home for, to be around his brothers, to be able to bare your soul without fear of being reprimanded or get into an altercation.

Tonight was necessary for all three of them, each fighting their struggle but all needing one another to make it through. Love comes in many forms, and tonight they showed one another they loved each other without saying the word.

26

Unwished-For-News

*E*ero sits in his office; he is considered the watchdog for the city. His job is to make sure money is not wasted, there is no fraud being committed nor abused.

Although he does not control whether projects are approved or not approved, he always pays special attention to anything that has to do with his old, historically black neighborhoods throughout the city. He is very much about being fair, but rather it is within how dollars are distributed between neighborhoods, or how nationalities and races are treated differently in the workplace.

In some ways, he's as passionate about being fair as he is about where the money goes and is spent. As a result, he developed relationships with city council people to lend an ear for areas he feels need improvement. He made sure to develop such relationship over his tenure as City Controller with Councilman Anderson from his old neighborhood, the Hill District, to send building and construction requests to his office.

He takes the afternoon to peruse the hallways of various councilpersons, and his final stop is at Councilman Anderson's office.

"Councilman Anderson, it's been a few weeks, how are things going?" asks Eero.

Councilman Lloyd Anderson has quite a reputation throughout the city. He has been the Hill District's councilman for over 30 years. He has always had a robust plan, pushed for money to come into the neighborhood way before it was in vogue to do so with efforts to stop regentrification.

He was alive for the riots that ran through the neighborhood; he saw outsiders from other neighborhoods come and firebomb black-owned businesses, then read in the newspapers the following day with the finger pointed at his people as the culprits. That impacted a young kid; he began as a public servant as a young adult. He finally realized the most significant impact would be made at the local level and focused on working for organizations that helped the city and neighborhoods.

Eventually, he caught the bug, went into politics, and proudly served for the last two decades. He is well respected and connected. When any Mayor wants to get through the city council, they speak to Councilman Anderson first, period. And if they don't the first time, they learn quickly after that he runs the show. They can either work with him or not, but as he says, so goes the council.

An overweight man, he is of average height with a salt and pepper goatee. He loves cigars and frequents Kolby's on Thursday nights for the special, whatever it might be that week. He is of the people but does not show much favoritism towards anyone; he tries to be fair in his dealings and appeals to help his district and the other districts.

"Mr. Eero Williams, it's a pleasure as always sir. Close that door behind you," Councilman Anderson says, waving his hand at his visitor.

Eero closes the door and takes a seat in front of his mahogany desk.

"I don't mind most of the advancements with not being able to do this and that but if I want to smoke a cigar in my own office, I think I should be able to do so," says Councilman Anderson as he takes out two cigars, clips them and hands one over to Eero.

"I have to agree with you on that one. What you have to drink with this fine cigar?"

"Just some bourbon sir."

"Sounds perfect."

Councilman Anderson and Eero toast one another, open the windows, light their cigars, lay back, and relax for a bit.

Eero loves these visits, but today, he has an agenda. "So, what's going on back in my old neighborhood?"

"First of all, you need to move back with your family so you can see for yourself, got those beautiful babies over in that bougie ass Squirrel Hill neighborhood," Councilman responds with a smile on his face showing the gap between his teeth, which he shows with pride anytime he can.

"In the next couple of months, we're going to develop the 2200 block of Webster Avenue. Build a few small 4-unit apartment complexes, have a small park there... it'll be a nice upgrade. That area has been an eye soar for a long time, it's time to upgrade that."

Eero quickly sits up, "Did you say the 2200 block of Webster Avenue?"

"Yes sir, I sure did."

Eero's entire body begins to tremble.

He places his drink down.

"I'll be right back, Councilman."

Eero quickly walks out of the office.

This particular proposal on the Hill District caught his attention this afternoon. The 2200 block on Webster Avenue has been a sore spot for many decades, with scant housing, mostly an empty lot with overgrown grass, a few abandoned cars, and nothing else. The proposal called for several townhouse units built, which would have some lower-income housing and commercial property.

The continuation of building up the neighborhood block by block, all the while displacing generations of families and forcing them to move farther out. This is all Eero sees when he reads the proposal in front of him.

Eero ponders for a moment, quickly gets up, and pulls up a map on his laptop. He quickly slams his laptop shut and calls his admin assistant.

"Whose proposal is for the 2200 block on Webster Avenue?"

"Let me take a look... that's Councilman Anderson's."

"Thank you."

Eero hangs up the phone, quickly gets out of the office, and walks into the bathroom as he is sweating profusely. He can feel his body temperature rising slowly but steadily. He grabs a few paper towels and wipes his face off, turns on the water and splashes it on his face.

He slowly closes his eyes and wipes the water from his face. The bathroom smell at the end of the day, piss on the floor, urinals not flushed, and overrun trash cans is making his stomach turn. Eero slides down the wall and sits on the floor. The echoes of honking horns and buses roaming a couple of stories below fill his eardrums; they sound as loud as thunder during a summer storm right now. Eero waits for a few moments and stands to his feet.

He rearranges his clothes, wipes his face, and quickly walks out of the bathroom and into Councilman Anderson's office.

"You look terrible kid...." the Councilman says.

"Yeah I don't know, something has hit me pretty hard. I'm going to head home," Eero says weakly.

"Let me know when you get there."

Eero nods and heads out.

"This shit can't be true, damn...." Eero says under his breath as he continues down the hallway towards the elevators.

27

Back in Business

After a one-week hiatus, the powers that be reinstates the Dr. Black Love show. The crew is back together, and Jameson is more fired up than ever. And not in a good way. He got some things on his chest that's been burning him up. Mic is hot.

"Keisha, welcome back."

"Dr. Black Love, nice to see you again."

"Abraham, welcome back as well."

Abraham gives a thumbs up.

"People we are back, and we are going even harder than ever. Many of you started hashtag campaigns for the show, called in, sent emails, letters even on our behalf, and I would like to personally thank you. I did not put out anything on social media on purpose, I wanted the people to bring the necessary attention to what you felt was wrong, and you did. We, the three of us, are grateful for that, and I wanted to take some time before we get into the show to say a few words."

Jameson gets comfortable in his chair.

"One thing I will never allow our show to do is apologize for speaking the truth. Right now in our current climate too many of us take someone's opinion about something and take it as the gospel. No research being conducted, no fact checking, and by that I mean actual fact checking, just oh he's on television or he's in the media, so let's take it as being factual and run with it.

One of the powerful things about social media is that everyone has a voice and what has turned into evil, in my opinion, is that everyone has a voice. If someone agrees with anything you do, then it has to be true."

Jameson continues, "With that being said, I said some things the other day that some have said are offensive and just my opinion. And to be very honest with you, I mix a little of both on this show, but what I say on this microphone will be my opinion based on facts that I have either experienced, witnessed or both.

What I said the other day was factual, look it up. And that's why I have not and will not apologize, period. They will walk me out of here before I acquiesce to any man that is scared to look at himself in the mirror when the truth presents itself."

"If nothing else, my audience can always bank on that from me. So, again the power of the people, the power of social media, all presented itself and we are back. Thank you, I promise you we will continue to do what we do here, which is help our fellow people, all people, and speak the truth.

Abraham please take us to a break, we will be back with Keisha and Dr. Black Love shortly."

Jameson puts down his headphones aggressively and sits there for a moment with the mean mug on; he's still pissed.

Jameson always had a very quick, mean streak inside him. Over the years he has learned to harness that anger and use his mind instead of his mouth to win his battles. His demeanor would not give it away, but he was always a person of action as opposed to talking.

The fact that he was only speaking into a microphone and not being more active was eating at him. His suspension allowed him to reflect on what got him to this point in his broadcasting career.

The people believed he cared, which he does... they believed he spoke the truth, which he does... and he was authentic, period. No matter how he felt someone would take his advice, he gave it to them straight.

He believed if he were honest with his audience, they would always be honest with him.

And the past week showed the powers that be that you can't hold down a locomotive for too long, and you better get on board or get run the fuck over —that's Jameson's memorandum operandum moving forward.

28

Swallow Your Pride

Kolby is riding around in his truck as he receives a call from Paul Romano. "Paul, what's going on, it's been a minute," Kolby says sarcastically.

"These types of things aren't done via text, you have to coordinate meetings, call backs, comb through details...."

"Right, and bill the hell out of me while you're at it," Kolby interrupts.

"You know I keep it modest with you Kolby."

"I'm fucking with you Paul, what you have for me."

"I feel like we're in a good place, that will avoid court time, and ultimately not make this a circus."

"How much does she want? Just give it to me straight, the money is all this is about at this point."

"$150,000..."

"Got damn... six figures Paul?!"

"That's what we negotiated it down from a quarter million, these cases like this don't come cheap. Now if I thought we could beat them easily, I'd tell you to not even bother."

"So you don't think we have any chance if it goes to court?"

"Looking over all the communication you had with her, the back and forth text messages, it doesn't look good. It makes you look sloppy, which I know you aren't, but we all slip up sometimes."

"I definitely fucked this one up, shit. I should have just let her ass quit, then this would have never happened. She was starting to cause issues with the staff, with customers. It was never personal, Paul," Kolby exclaimed.

"Kolby, I know you. This will be water under the bridge at some point, a lesson learned. You are way smarter than I am, if you beat yourself up over this then she wins more than some money."

Kolby stops his truck in front of an apartment complex and turns off the keys.

"Yeah I hear you Paul."

"I even put in there to pay it off over a five year period... So I think you should take the deal, and be done with it."

"I'll call you Monday."

"OK, let me know first thing, if you have more questions over this weekend, then just give me a call," Paul says.

"Talk to you then."

Kolby hangs up the phone.

Kolby's family that he rarely speaks to are not what most would consider upstanding citizens. As much as his mother kept him away from his other family, he knows them and of what they are capable. From petty theft, bank robberies, murder, his family has done it all.

And as a younger Kolby once said, "You have to keep some gangsters around you, you never know." Occasionally these relationships can come in handy, and if one has enough money, things can get handled swiftly, and for much less than $150,000.

Kolby touches the dash and stares at the screen of phone numbers.

Less than 100 feet away, his cousin can make any problems disappear and without any hiccups. The money was not his main issue; the worker was extorting him, he committed no crime, he did nothing wrong outside of morally being involved with one of his workers. And now the penalty for that would cost him $150,000.

Kolby touches the screen and dials Jameson.

"What up bruh," answers Jameson.

"Just got the details on the negotiations with the case."

"Don't seem like you're too happy about it."

"Buck fifty, it'll cost me over 5 years."

Jameson knows Kolby well, so he takes his time with him.

"Let's think about this for a moment...." Jameson says.

"Jameson, I don't want to have one of your infamous breakdowns at the moment."

"Yeah you do, that's why your ass called me," Jameson says matter of factly. He knows his friend, and he is about to do something stupid.

Kolby chuckles to himself, "I fucking hate you sometimes. Go ahead and break it down."

"Let's be honest, you start fucking a waitress at your lounge, then you wifey her right?" Jameson goes in.

"You know I don't give titles."

"She thought she was your girl and you didn't tell her she wasn't. Therefore, you and I both know how women are... She was your girlfriend."

Jameson continues, "Then you carry on enough for your staff not to find out. You get tired of her because... that's you, break it off, and then she gets lazy and sloppy at work. Am I correct so far?"

"Spot on as always, please proceed."

"You fire her, months later comes the lawsuit. Now, you have to pay the piper for making a mistake. Sometimes we can swindle out of them, sometimes you have to pay."

"As much as I appreciate your little soliloquy that's not exactly why I called you."

"My apologies, I just know you can get off track, so I wanted to make sure you was on point."

"Right, so I'm outside of Big Ray's spot."

"Your cousin?" Jameson asks with one eyebrow raised.

"Yeah."

"Come on Kolby... first of all we not going into details on the horn but leave that shit alone. Yeah it's some money, but it's not nearly as bad as it can be if you go down that path."

"It'll be over with."

"You never know, all it takes is one mishap and everything you've built up for is gone, period. There won't be no come back story, nothing. You'll just be another dumb nigger that got some money and couldn't leave the hood behind."

Kolby stares out the window. Jameson's words resonate with a part of him that they have all battled with since choosing to go down the right path. If you backslide one time and it backfires, everything you have done to that point will be an afterthought, and you become a statistic. A lifetime of work up in smoke, and the world will turn the page.

"This is some bullshit, Jameson," Kolby soaks in his pity.

"It is... but you have to swallow your pride sometimes. Just leave, it's not worth it bruh," Jameson pleads.

Kolby starts up his truck and pulls off.

"I could have had a hell of a night in Vegas with $150,000."

"That's some expensive pussy...Think about that next time and just say no."

"Damn right, I'll holla at you. Appreciate it."

"Later."

They both hang up the phone.

29

Flexing Muscle

E ero is sitting in a chair reading while getting makeup applied. He has a couple of minutes before he leaves for his interview.

Mary is seated across from him, going over some note cards, writing and editing them, and as she finishes one, she hands it over to Eero.

Eero has always been a tactical wizard; he rarely fights with the same weapons thrown at him. Instead, his opponent has taken to ads that continue to spew negativity and lies about his track record and past.

Initially, the team had come up with a strategy to blast his opponent right back with factual information about himself and his office. That showed some positive signs, but as the election grew closer, he wanted to give a final blow to his opponent. Now was his opportunity to speak directly to the people on a recorded interview that would allow him to set the record straight, control the circumstances, and ultimately the narrative of what was being said about him.

Eero reads more notecards from Mary; he missed these moments when they would work together as a team. Rarely did they get alone time, and even this evening was not exactly a date night, but it was important for his campaign. Mary was schooled by her father in dealing with the public, bouncing from meeting to meeting, taking notes, and then discussing the finer details on car rides home.

Although Eero felt that Mary leaned too heavily on her family at times, she has taught him a lot in business and even more so in dealing with people. Eero was not very polished when they first started dating in high school. However, as he showed more and more promise, he was allowed into the inner circles that Mary's father ran in, a rare thing for a young man, much less a man of color, to do in this city.

Eero attempted to rely less and less on Mary's family as he continued through his career. He wanted to establish himself as an individual, not be known simply as a son-in-law with good connections. So now Eero was doing one of his first major breakaways without the consent of his father-in-law. He was a bit nervous but felt good about the move; if nothing else, it was his strategy, and the fallout would be all on him.

The interview he felt would give him a one-on-one opportunity to say everything he needed to say. In addition, KDKA has a big following, and he would be featured on the evening news the next day; the bulk of his interview would then be shown throughout the days remaining up until the election, both online and in purchased ads on the network. Thus, a multi-faceted strategy would deliver for voters on various platforms and give him the necessary push to win the election.

Mary was unusually quiet outside of her scribbling notes and talking under her breath while reading the note cards.

"You think I'm making a mistake?" Eero asks, looking at his beloved wife. Tonight, she looks different, but he can't put his finger on it.

"I don't know what to think, you aren't including me on any strategy," Mary snaps back at the question.

"You told me you didn't want to be involved, now you say I don't tell you enough. I can't win with you sometimes."

"You just don't get it Eero, you did not have to make this campaign so hard on yourself."

"I don't want to be under your father's thumb all the time, we can do this on our own," Eero says defiantly.

"This is not about who gets credit, it's about winning, period. You either win or lose, Eero. There are not participation medals given out in politics."

"I'm not going to lose. That's why we're here tonight."

"I just hope you know what you're doing."

"Damn right I do...."

Mary rolls her eyes and continues to read the notecard, and writes down more notes.

"Here," Mary hands Eero the notecard.

Eero reads the notecard, and at the very end of the card, it says, "Be the best because you are. Love, Mary."

That was the phrase Mary said to Eero as he was coming up in his career. Back then, they were so close; they would spend hours together alone and not care. Now they are not able to spend ten minutes alone without arguing.

Eero closes his eyes and breathes deeply.

Mary stands up and grabs her purse.

"Where are you going?" asks Eero.

"Home, you don't need me here."

"Yes, yes I do. Please sit."

Mary slowly sits down and stares at Eero.

"I know that things are rocky between us, and I take blame for some of that. I don't take the time out to see how you feel, check in on your day, I haven't been the most attentive husband lately and I'm sorry for that... I do love you, that has not changed one bit. I have just taken things for granted and not been attentive enough to us."

"It's not all your fault Eero, but what can we do now?"

"Very simple, we just have to make the effort, that's it. Make the effort to spend time together, talk, go on a date."

"We don't have time for that."

"We have to make time."

Mary nods in agreement.

"I do appreciate you being here, I appreciate you always being here for me."

"I know you do, just go out there and be yourself, that's good enough to beat anyone."

Eero grabs Mary's hands and kisses them with his eyes closed. "I love you Mary."

Eero turns to walk away, but Mary grabs him.

"Kiss your wife."

Eero smiles, and they kiss one another. "Make sure you're here when I get back."

Mary nods in agreement. "I'm not going anywhere."

30

Night To Celebrate

*J*ameson, Eero, and Kolby are enjoying a night at Kolby's lounge. Eero has decisively won his election tonight, guaranteeing him another four years as Pittsburgh's Controller.

Recently Kolby settled his civil case, and despite losing money, he did not admit to any wrongdoing and ultimately only lost money.

Jameson's show has taken off since his suspension. Sponsorship on the show is up; he now has a publicist to handle his requests for appearances. In addition, he has gained national recognition for the unique spin on the show supporting black people, which has been ignored quite often by the mainstream.

Tonight is a celebration of the culmination of the adversity each of them faced.

Over the past few months, they have all dealt with tremendous stress, overcome obstacles, and stood strong in the face of adversity. Each has had each other's back, supported one another, and lived up to the mantra of being their brother's keeper.

The vibe in the lounge is lively; the DJ is playing old-school hip hop, drinks are in abundance, the people of the city are out in full force with plenty of smiles going around.

Kolby is in his glory; he loves a crowd, he loves to make money, and he loves to be the center of attention. All three of these desires are being met tonight. He works the room, giving dap to every male and a hug to each woman he comes in contact with. He introduces himself, as if he needs an introduction, and makes sure everyone feels at home.

Eero and Jameson are sitting at the bar laughing at their friend; they don't seek the spotlight and are comfortable letting Kolby soak in the celebrity he has attained.

"Jameson, I need to thank you," Eero says.

"For what?"

"A couple months ago when Mary came over to speak to you. Initially I was a little annoyed, not because she spoke to you but more because you had to be thrown in the middle of our shit."

"There isn't a married couple that hasn't had some type of issues, and like I always said, you two are my favorite couple. If you two don't make it, I have no hope."

They toast one another and drink.

"What you need to do is finally get things right with Ryann before someone else takes your place."

Eero points over to Ryann, who is walking back with Mary but keeps getting stopped by random men. She politely ignores them, but the point being she is a hot commodity.

"We're coming up on six months soon...."

"Come on with that bullshit."

"Something is gonna happen, it always does. Not saying I want it to but watch, some shit is gonna change things. That's just my luck," Jameson says with a hint of sadness in his voice.

"You don't even believe in luck?" Eero asks.

"Not with love I don't, that's for damn sure."

"Just don't let her slip through your hands, make that work."

Mary and Ryann come over to the bar.

"Surprised you made it back Ryann, all those guys trying to swoon down on you," says Jameson.

Ryann rolls her eyes.

"I have no time for any of these lames in here."

"Let's do a shot, for Eero's victory today."

"Hell no, not tonight," Mary echos.

"That's exactly why we're doing it."

Jameson goes behind the bar, grabs four shot glasses, pours Patron, grabs four lemons, and heads back over.

"Mary, love you but you gotta do it. We won tonight, you have to celebrate if you're out."

Mary waves to give her a glass.

"Before we drink, Eero please give us a few words," exclaims Jameson.

Eero slowly picks up the shot glass and holds it into the air.

"To keep it simple tonight, I am thankful to be here with the most important people in my life. My beautiful wife, my best friends and close friends. Here's to four more years of prosperity and love."

Everyone holds the glasses in the air, and they all toast and drink. Eero kisses Mary, and they hug one another.

"They're so damn cute," says Ryann.

"They are, I agree," Jameson says in response.

The party continues into the early morning hours; eventually, Kolby's closes, but they go upstairs into the office for a night cap. The men are playing pool while the ladies are seated on the couch.

"Jameson, when the hell are you going to wife up Ryann is what I want to know?" asks Kolby loud enough so Ryann could hear.

"When are you going to have a girlfriend that you actually bring around us, worrying about my shit?" Jameson responds while laughing.

"I am not the marrying type bruh," Kolby shoots back.

"You know what, you are right about that," says Eero.

"With all due respect to you, Eero and your marriage, I don't get the marriage thing. I barely like a woman for more than a month, why the hell would I want to be tied down forever to one woman."

"Is that a question or a statement?" asks Jameson.

"Fuck you, it's both how about that," Kolby fires back.

"You don't give a woman long enough to even show you that she's worth keeping around," Eero chimes in.

"Cause I already know how I am. I will be like this until I leave this earth, no point in changing now."

"Marriage is hard work, it's not easy but I am happy to be married even with the ups and downs," says Eero.

"What is the point of marriage?" Kolby asks Eero.

"There's no one answer to that. Everyone has to have their own goals. Your goals need to align and when they do, it can be special. Now when they don't align, you have problems."

"Do you believe that we have one person made for us in the world? Like literally one person is destined to be with you, and that's it?" Jameson asks.

"Yes!" Ryann shouts from the other side of the room.

Everyone busts out laughing.

"See, here she go...." Jameson points at Ryann.

"How are things with you and Jameson?" Mary asks Ryann.

"Pretty good, we're in a good place right now. He's just scared of failing."

"Yeah aren't we all to some extent. It's not like anyone gets married to get divorced, but keeping the train moving in the right direction is very difficult."

"You and Eero have been together so long, how do you do it?"

"We have had our ups and downs, just like anyone else. But I know his heart, he loves our family and he loves me. And more than anything, I trust him."

"When he looked at you tonight when he did the toast, I could tell he loved you. I want Jameson to look at me like that, or someone if it isn't him."

They both laugh.

"All jokes aside, you can just tell when a man is really in love with his wife. And he is."

"We've had a lot of years to get to that point. And all the years have not been good, trust me."

"In the bad times what makes you fight through it?"

"Because I know he will fight through it also. Now sometimes I have to shake his ass up, but when he's focused he's pretty awesome."

"Maybe he can rub off on Jameson," Ryan says looking over at her boyfriend.

"Jameson is a good brotha, he's just allowed himself to hide behind this character he made and his ex, and her dumb shit."

Ryann stares over at Jameson.

"Don't worry too much about anything, he knows you and what he has with you."

"He mentioned you and his ex were kind of close."

"At one point we were, I mean we would see them a lot. You kind of become close because these three are not ever going to be around one another. But at this point I don't speak to her much, we're their daughters God-parents so we do our best to stay present."

Ryann is quiet.

"I want to thank you for helping us with the interview at KDKA. That was huge for the campaign."

"You're welcome, Eero is awesome at his job, it was a no-brainer to help. Did you ever tell him you made the call?" Ryann asks.

"Nope, you learn sometimes to let a man's ego just run with it. He thinks it's because he's so amazing, which he is. But I let him run with it."

They both toast one another's wine glasses and have a drink.

The three continue their conversation...

"I don't know, it's a tough one there. There's like seven or eight billion people on earth. No way we are pre-destined to be with one person," Kolby says.

"My perspective has always been that we are placed in situations where we make choices that impact our lives in a big way. Not every day, but if you think back there are choices that impact what we eventually end up doing, who we end up with, where we live, all those things." Eero says.

Eero continues, "For instance Jameson, what if you never went out west. Like the decision for you to go led to you having Zanita, getting married and divorced, but if you didn't go your life would be way different."

"Very true, that's a really good point, Eero. I can think of three, four things that really shaped my life and the choices in those decisions were huge even if you didn't know at that time," Jameson says.

"Enough with all this philosophical shit, I have to make a toast before the night is over," Kolby says.

Kolby moves halfway between the pool table and couch.

"Look, I know I'm a little inebriated but I do have something to say. We've all been through some shit the last few months. We leaned on each other, we argued, we listened, we cried, we had some tough conversations. Ultimately the most important thing is we stayed together.

Eero and Jameson, you two are my brothers, through everything and any time I need you, you're there. Love y'all more than I can express.

So raise a glass for Eero and Mary for winning that campaign, raise a glass for Jameson and lighting up the radio waves on your new show, raise a glass for me getting through this case. And I have to say, Jameson, you better lock in what you have."

Jameson gives a thumbs up in response, and they all raise their glasses and toast.

31

Not in the Plans

*F*ameson is putting together Zanita's room. He has
fully furnished the bedroom from the bed, the
matching bedroom set of her favorite color purple,
two matching nightstands and a matching dresser,
fully stocked closet with new clothes, even though she will only
be in town for a week. He is a bit nervous as he wants
everything to be perfect. She has to love the room as soon as
she sees it.

Jameson is on FaceTime with Ryann.

"How does it look Ryann?" Jameson scans the room with his
phone.

"Everything looks great, you did a great job Daddy J!"

"You helped tremendously, I appreciate it. Thank you very much, it means a lot to me," Jameson says and he smiles and scans the room with his eyes. He's so excited to see his little girl.

"You're welcome, but no need to thank me. She's the most important person in the world to you, so I had to help you."

"I want her to be happy...."

"You could have a cardboard box in there and she'd still be happy," Ryann teases.

"You don't know her very well yet but I know what you mean."

"I can't wait to meet her."

"Me neither, thank you again. Let me get ready and I will call you later."

"Enjoy your night with your daughter, don't worry about calling me. Good night."

"Good night."

Jameson is anxiously waiting by the door and looking out the peephole. He sees Charlotte and Zanita, and he immediately opens the door.

"Z, I missed you so much."

Jameson picks up Zanita, and they both hold each other tightly. Then, he lifts and carries her in and continues to hug her.

"Daddy, I love you."

"Love you too dear. Hey, I want to show you your room."

Jameson puts down Zanita and goes over to Charlotte.

"Thank you for bringing her Charlotte."

Charlotte nods in agreement.

Jameson takes Zanita into her room, and she lets out a squeal that can crack windows. He loves that sound.

"It's so pretty Daddy!!" jumping up and down in excitement. She doesn't know where to start, so she runs all around, checking out her new room.

Charlotte, sister of Camryn, former sister-in-law of Jameson, almond complexion, beautiful teeth, hair is always on point, and flawless. Dressed inappropriate attire for the fall, not too heavy but enough to keep you warm at night.

She and Jameson had always had a good relationship; even when Camryn and Jameson were going through their divorce, she always advocated for him. Jameson felt she was always fair and honest, which allowed him to trust her with Zanita more than just about anyone in the world.

Her demeanor was not as upbeat as usual, considering they had not seen one another in nearly a year, typically she is lively and talkative, but tonight she is melancholy.

Jameson comes out of the room and notices Charlotte is sitting on the couch staring off into the night skies.

"Charlotte, thank you for driving up and bringing Z, I can't thank you enough."

"You know it's no problem, she needs to see you. She talked about you the entire drive up here," Charlotte says dryly, trying to smile.

"That's my girl. What's going on though, you're really quiet?" Jameson sounds concerned.

"If you go in the hallway, you'll see why."

Jameson looks puzzled but goes into the hallway and sees eight bags. He turns around and comes back in.

"Why the hell are there eight bags out there Charlotte?"

Charlotte gets up and hands Jameson a note.

"It's from my lovely sister. I'll go check on Z, we can talk when she goes to sleep."

Jameson reads...

Jameson, the past five months have been too much for me. I can't do this on my own anymore. We can figure things out, but for now, you have to take the reins. I know this wasn't our plan, but you have your family back home and more support. Z doesn't know, and I'd hope we can talk, and both tell her. I'm sorry. Camryn.

Jameson was caught between being excited and irate. Part of him felt better knowing he would not have to worry about whether Zanita was being cared for properly or getting the attention she needed. But the other side of him can't help but feel that Camryn is doing this out of resentment or some sadistic plot to bring him down when he is finally reaching the heights he planned years ago with his career.

Of course, we all have flaws, but Camryn's biggest flaw was her not being able to be unselfish in Jameson's eyes. He could never quite grasp if it were intentional or unintentional, but he always had to battle her thinking of herself first and everyone else afterward.

It was a challenging course to navigate in dealing with her while they were together, and it has multiplied now that they are apart. Jameson heard her complaints about things being more difficult, he solicited help from other individuals he knew, but that would never replace what he did. Now that Camryn reneged on their deal, he was left to pick up the pieces and deal with the consequences, basically overnight and with no heads up.

Jameson put the note down and walked into Zanita's bedroom.

Later that night, Jameson walks out of Zanita's bedroom. Charlotte is having a drink of red wine at the table.

"She finally went to sleep?" she asks dryly.

Jameson sits at the table.

"Your sister is, is...."

"Yes I know. I didn't know about it either until a few boxes showed up before she arrived the other day. I didn't think anything about it but when I picked them up and brought them to my house that's the first thing she opened up. What did the note say?"

"She can't do it, and I have more help here basically. We said a year, this is well short of that. I have worked really hard on not expecting her to be what she isn't. I think we focus on that too much in these situations but her inability to be a real mother is impacting my ability to be the best father that I can be."

"I'm sorry Jameson, I can help you out as much as I can," Charlotte is always so supportive. Her sister can be a pill, she knows all too well.

"You're four hours away in Maryland. I don't expect you to uproot your life to help us."

"That's what family does for each other. Z is obviously my niece but you will always be my family."

"I appreciate that."

"What's your plan going to be? You have your show in the evening, she will have school during the day, how will you do it?"

"I have no idea, I'll figure it out though, and we'll be fine."

"You always have to save the day with her, I don't know how you put up with it," Charlotte says shaking her head and taking another sip of wine.

"Truthfully that's one of the reasons I left, for her to have to step up to the plate, but she could only do that for five months. Z will be better off here anyway."

"I think so too."

"You know she asked if we could tell her together, like we decided to do this. She did this all on her own, she's such a selfish asshole."

"Jameson, you are the best person to have Zanita in the entire world. You are her world, and she is yours. This wasn't in your plan but sometimes we have to make lemonade from lemons."

Jameson nods in agreement and slowly stands up from the table.

"Make sure you finish that bottle off since you opened it."

They both smile at each other.

"Take my bed, I'm gonna sleep with Z."

"Hell no, the last thing you need is one of your girls finding my hair in your bed. I'll take the couch."

"You always got some smart shit to say. Love you."

"Love you too," and she did. He's a good dude.

Jameson goes into the bedroom and gently crawls into bed with Zanita. The juxtaposition of his feelings was enormous right now. His soul felt complete now that Zanita was back with him. He could hold her, kiss her and be in her presence every single day.

But, on the other hand, his disdain for her mother could not be at a higher point. Not only did he feel that she was abandoning her duties as a mother, but she also did it without discussing anything with him and left her sister to do the dirty work. It took everything in his power to keep his blood from boiling over, calling her and saying every negative thought that had ever crept into his mind about her.

But, ultimately, he felt that would hurt his daughter and let her know that she was getting to him, so he passed on the thought. Instead, he would enjoy the moment for the night holding his daughter.

32

Again, Never

J ameson is sitting on a bench at the Point. He asked Ryann to meet him so they can talk. He is unusually jittery and nervous about this interaction that is about to transpire. The sun is shining brightly, and the point is buzzing with people jogging, lying out tanning, walking, and just enjoying the rarely seen clear day in Pittsburgh.

Ryann walks up, and they embrace one another and sit together.

"I remember these benches, you always came down here to get away," Ryann says to Jameson, looking around and taking in the view.

"More to think by Khaled and get away from everyone for sure."

"How did things go last night with Zanita?"

"Things went well, but I also got this from her sister," Jameson says and hands the note over to Ryann, and she quickly reads it.

"I thought you two had an agreement?" Ryann looks bewildered.

"Just like all agreements, they are until they aren't. Part of me thinks this was on purpose and in her plans all along, just when things are really starting to get going, she does this. Kind of feels premeditated," Jameson says staring off into the water before him.

"I guess most people think of their ex in a negative way but maybe she's telling the truth..." Ryann wants to believe what she just said, but what can she say in this moment? Damned if you do, damned if you don't... she's still the mother of his daughter. *Careful Ryann.*

"Maybe, ultimately it throws everything off in life and I just wanted things here to be perfect before Z came out here permanently. Now I have to figure out everything, arrange for childcare, school, get her winter clothes, a coat—all that shit."

"I can help you with that."

"I'm nervous about that too, she's never met anyone I've dated."

"You weren't dating before Jameson."

"Touché."

Jameson continues, "I really have no idea how to introduce you, like what do I say, how do I explain who we are...."

Ryann smiles at Jameson.

"Why are you smiling, I'm really serious."

"At times you remind me of the 16-year-old version of yourself. Your mannerisms, the way you get flustered... it's cute."

"I appreciate the nostalgia but that isn't helping me right now."

"My point was we figured it out with kid problems, which are nothing, and we're grown now. Zanita will love anyone you love dear, and we won't do anything that makes her feel odd or weird."

Jameson looks out at the water and is quiet for a moment.

"The night before I left, I cried like a baby. I can't even tell you the last time I cried but that night I did. Ever since she was born every move I made was about her, no matter how big or small it was always how it would impact Zanita.

And this move was about a lot of things but it was the first time I did not put her first. It was better in all other aspects of life, career wise, spiritually, emotionally, everything. But I felt such enormous guilt about leaving, like I would not be able to protect her anymore, or be there to wipe a tear away if she cried. I almost didn't go."

"Why did you?"

Jameson turns and looks at Ryann.

"It was the right thing to do, when things fall into place like everything did about coming back, I knew it was the right thing to do. And knowing she would be here in a year, it was the easiest hardest decision I ever made. Now what I did not expect is to find you when I got back here much less end up falling for you again."

"That's the truth there, I never expected that either. But what we have now is good, I don't believe we smother each other, we don't demand too much of one another's time, and the respect is there. I know with your daughter being here it will take away from some of our time, but I want to be there with you and her, eventually," Ryann says softly and reassuringly.

"I don't know how long that's going to take Ryann. I'm nervous about that."

"I'm not going anywhere, Jameson. You aren't going to try to sneak out the back door and leave me again. That's not happening."

Jameson looks perplexed.

"So if I said I wanted to end things you wouldn't respect that?"

"I would respect what you said but not pay attention to it."

"Well damn, you kind of sound like me."

They both laugh with one another.

"I know that she's an amazing little girl and it would be very special for her to see someone like yourself, what you do career wise, how to move in a crowd, how you are just an amazing woman...."

"It would be an honor to help the princess along her path."

"Well so much for my break-up speech...."

Ryann hits Jameson on the arm.

"I'm joking!"

Jameson grabs Ryann, and they kiss.

"Thank you for not running away from me."

"I'm not running anywhere, I'm here with you step by step," Ryann replies.

33

Conversation With the Courier (Part 2)

*J*ameson is being interviewed again by Adam Franklin.

"Mr. Clarkson I wasn't sure if we'd get a second exclusive with you sir. I appreciate you giving us the opportunity," says Adam.

"I will always make time for our paper here in the city. You all wanted to speak to me when nobody else did, I will never forget that."

"We want to focus on other areas this time. Your show is doing great, there is an amazing buzz in the city and all over the country for that matter. Why do you feel your show has grown so much in maybe six months?" Adam inquires and Jameson pauses before he responds…

"I feel the station has done a great job of marketing the show, and I have to admit that it gave us a platform to do what do we do and reach more people than we've ever been able to do alone. And then, we're unique and honest. It's as simple as that, we're true to our audience and they appreciate it," says Jameson.

"A couple months ago, there was some tension there with your suspension after some so-called controversial statements. How did you feel going through that situation?"

Jameson expected this question, "I was initially pissed off because I didn't and still do not feel that I said anything controversial. I was just telling the truth, an uncomfortable truth to some, but still the truth. It just shows you that certain people only care when it's hitting a nerve for them. Biggest thing out of that for me was the support from our audience, it was unreal. They bombarded the station, hitting up anyone that would listen, they had us trending online for like the entire week. Just shows you that the real power is with the people. It was beautiful and we appreciate it still to this day," says Jameson proud as ever of his city. What a welcome home!

"Now that you've been back for some time now, how do you feel about the move and being back home?"

"It's been a blessing, truly. I am better spiritually, emotionally, my mind is clear, I am at ease. There's stress every day, just living is stressful to a certain point, but when you're in the right place, you can feel it internally. I rarely use this word but it's been damn near a perfect decision to this point."

"That's great, nothing like having peace of mind. What things do you have in store for the show, I mean without giving up too much intel at least?" asks Adam.

"Right now things are in a good place, we do small things here and there just to test things out. It would be foolish for us to make any significant moves at this point."

"How do you feel Keisha has helped the show? You two seem to have great chemistry and it actually seems real, not fake. There is a lot of that going on with radio and TV as you know."

"Very true, I've witnessed it. A crew will sound great on the air but horrible off the air, and it always blows up at some point. Keisha and I have really hit it off as co-hosts. She has great ideas, she speaks her mind, she gives the show a woman's perspective that was never there before. And now I have someone to argue with when necessary," Jameson smiles, and they both laugh.

"What about your personally, I heard through the grapevine you will be doing some things for the community, not sure if you can speak on those or not?" Adam probes a little.

"I believe I can to a certain extent, not too many details. It's funny the only person I had to answer to when I moved here was myself. Now I have a publicist, a manager, my daughter and my girlfriend to answer to. These four women run my life, period. To answer your question, there will be some programs that I am spearheading to help children with broadcasting, learning how to brand, some other areas of the industry as well. Again, I can't go into too many details, but it will be focused on kids, I love working with kids."

"Why is that?" asks Adam.

"They're just beautiful, they have so much heart, willpower, they feel that they can do anything. We lose that as adults, we allow ourselves to settle for being average. You never say to yourself, I'm going to shoot for the middle in anything in life but most of us settle for middle class, a decent house, some money. Kids believe they will have everything they think of, regardless of how outlandish it is. We all need that, we all need to just go for it. That's what I get out of working with kids, I love that," says Jameson with passion and zeal. His eyes sparkling with hope and aspiration for the future generation.

"I have to say you seem so much livelier, your energy is contagious brother. I am so happy for your success, please keep it up."

"For you to see it means it's glowing, and that's a good thing. Thank you for the support and I look forward to speaking to you again."

Jameson and Adam shake hands.

34

About To Get Real

Eero is going through the approved projects for the next few months. The council has approved the project for building on the 2200 block of Webster Avenue, and it's just a matter of time.

Eero begins to feel nauseous; this is a road he does not want to travel down. So much time has passed, yet the gut-wrenching pain is still fresh, as if it happened yesterday.

He will have to tell Jameson and Kolby, and he does not feel good about that conversation, and how it will impact them moving forward.

Eero picks up his phone, goes into the group message for the three of them, and begins to type...but he pauses....

The project isn't going to start immediately, so he stops short of sending the message.

Eero is the least confrontational; he prefers to work around things, figure them out, and then go for it. If he can avoid collateral damage in his mind, it's even all the better.

This current situation has him stuck; he has nobody to bounce ideas off of, Mary will not understand, nobody will. He will have to deal with the torture and pain for a little longer on his own....

35

Invaluable Asset

Since Zanita's arrival, Jameson has set things up rather nicely. They wake up around 6:30 a.m., eat breakfast, relax some, and drop her off at school by 8 a.m.; she gets out at 2 p.m., a nanny picks her up, and they walk home from her downtown school.

His show starts at 3 p.m., so they usually are in the office by at least 1:30 p.m., and it ends at 7 p.m., so he never gets out before 8 p.m. Every night he calls her twice during his show on FaceTime during breaks, and he gets home by 8:30 p.m. to put her in bed by 9 p.m., rinse and repeat each day during the week.

Zanita struggled some adjusting to her new school, schedule, the weather, and just not seeing her mother as much. But as kids typically do, she adapted and is now adjusted in her routine. She has new friends, enjoys the seasons, and is very happy and in a great routine.

Today is not a typical day. Jameson receives a message from his nanny that she is not able to make it today. A family emergency has come up, and the timing could not be worse. Jameson is in the office, he came downtown to eat lunch with Ryann, and his pre-show meeting is about to start. He does not like asking his parents to drive, Eero is nowhere to be found, and he would ask Kolby as an absolute last resort... But he could ask Ryann.

Ryann has adjusted well to Zanita, and Zanita has been willing to accept her as Daddy's friend to this point. But having her pick her up and spend hours with her alone is totally different. Unfortunately, he had limited options and time, so he has to ask.

He picks up his phone and dials.

"Hey there, how are you?" asks Ryann.

"Ryann, I need your help," replies Jameson.

"What's wrong?"

"The nanny called off today, it's damn near 1:30, we're about to do the pre-show, can you pick up Z today?" Jameson asks nervously.

"Of course I can. That's why you asked to put me on the list."

"I know but that was just in case shit happens."

"This is shit happening Jameson, I'm fine babe, you just worry about your show and I'll take care of the princess," Ryann says eagerly (and nervously but she would never let Jameson see that).

"Thank you so much, you have no idea... I thought I'd have to call Kolby," he laughs.

"Yeah I think she might be better off on her own than to do that."

They both laugh.

"He's not that bad, she'd just eat cereal and candy for dinner. He's like a teddy bear with kids."

"That's cause he's a kid his damn self," Ryann checks her watch. "Let me get out of here so I can meet her on time."

"Thank you, I really mean it."

"I know you do, good bye. It's time to focus, I got Zanita."

They both hang up.

Later that evening, Jameson unlocks his apartment and walks into the lovely aroma of chicken fettuccini Alfredo, one of his favorites. Ryann peeks from the kitchen and points to Zanita's bedroom. Jameson walks in and sees Zanita is already sleeping, holding on to one of her dolls. He goes over, kisses her on the forehead, and walks back out, closing the door slightly.

Jameson places his bag on the table and gives Ryann a bouquet.

"What is this for?" asks Ryann.

"Just saying thank you, I know you love flowers so I figured it would at least somewhat make up for you losing an evening."

She grabs the flowers and kisses Jameson.

"They're beautiful, thank you dear."

"You're welcome, how did it go this evening? She's already sleeping, what did you do, give her some damn Benadryl?" Jameson teases his girlfriend. He sees her efforts and he appreciates that. This is new for him.

Ryann throws her wet towel at him.

"No crazy... we ate dinner, we read a book, she took a bath and she was tired. So we laid down for a few moments and she was sleep."

"It was that easy huh, it never goes like that with me."

"That's because you don't have a woman's touch. It's just natural for us."

"I'm impressed, and the food smells delicious."

"Your food is in the oven."

"You out here like a wife, you go girl."

"I hate you... do you want something to eat or not?"

"Yes please."

While Jameson is eating, they continue discussing the evening.

"How was she when you picked her up?"

"She was a little thrown off by not seeing the nanny. But she was fine, we walked across the bridge, and had a good conversation. That girl can talk."

Jameson smiles and laughs.

"Yes she can."

"She asked me some interesting questions. One was how did we meet? And I told her we knew each other from high school... and she asked me if we ever kissed before? I told her a long time ago way before she was born...."

"Damn, I apologize but kids say what they think."

"That's not all, she asked if I was going to be Daddy's new wife."

"Oh shit, what did you say?"

"I told her that was up to Daddy," Ryann winks and gets up from the table.

Jameson looks at her and tilts his head in a manner that suggests he senses some fabrication.

"That's your daughter?"

"She didn't ask you that."

Ryann stops and turns, "Oh yes, she definitely did."

"How did she respond to that?"

"She stopped for a second and then nodded her head, and said Daddy likes you and kept it moving."

"She's a smart girl, Daddy does like you. Can you come back over here for a moment?"

Ryann sits again.

"I know it's Wednesday but on Friday evening my parents are having dinner, they invited us to come over. My mother just asked me today, but this is big. Like it's actually my mother and father and us all eating together."

"I thought your parents hated each other... what happened?"

"Zanita happened... every time we go over there she makes my dad come upstairs, and over the last month or so it's like they like each other again. I don't know what happened or what she did, but it's really cool."

"I'd be honored to go, I haven't seen them in forever," Ryann says.

"My dad will love to see you, I think he wants you more than I do."

"I am stunningly beautiful and single...."

"You aren't single."

Ryann looks around the room.

"What was that Mr. Clarkson?"

"I said you aren't single, you heard what I said."

"Are you saying you're my man now Jameson?"

"Do I really have to say it."

"Yes."

Jameson walks over to the other side of the table. "Ms. Davis, do you want to be my girlfriend, yes or no?"

"I'd be honored."

They kiss one another; Jameson picks Ryann up and carries her into the bedroom.

36

Showtime (Part 4)

"**D**r. Black Love, I saved this one just for this moment of the show. I don't think it's a topic we've hit since we began our new show here. And I believe you're going to go in on this one," Keisha proclaims.

"You're making me nervous, last time we had all these proclamations we was off the air for a week," Jameson replies jokingly. They all laugh.

"Very funny, you've had jokes all night. Tonight we're doing it a little different."

"How so?"

"Live call in, we will do this once a week moving forward. And we will have follow up calls to see how things are going as well. How do you feel about that?" Keisha asks her co-host.

"I love it, we've talked about that for some months now. It's a totally new way to interact so let's do it!" Jameson is pleased and excited to get going. His vision is living out right before his eyes.

"Our caller today is from the state of Maryland, we will not use her real name of course. She is going to read her letter that she sent in, then you can ask her questions and most importantly give her advice, Dr. Black Love," Keisha spurts out the rules. Sexy.

"Excellent, let's get it started," Jameson rubs his hands together as if preparing for a delicious meal.

"Please read young lady," Keisha says to the caller.

A female voice comes on the air and says, "Dear Dr. Black Love, I am in a bad situation. I was married to my high school sweetheart; we were both 25-years-old. We have two amazing babies, one boy, and one girl. We stayed married for seven years, and then it ended. I didn't work when our kids were born; he had an outstanding career in advertising. He was intelligent, focused, and driven. He traveled a lot, I was home with the kids, and that's when our problems started. There were many reasons but mainly because he kept cheating, over and over again. Finally, I couldn't take it anymore, and I left. The thing about it was he took care of us all; we made good money and lived in a nice neighborhood with a four-bedroom house, three-car garage out in the suburbs.

When I left all that left also, I was back in the city, struggling with my two kids. Their father paid child support and he is amazing with the kids, but I struggled to start over with a career. Eventually, I got on my feet, got a townhouse, and we're doing all right. Not as good as before, but we're in a good place.

Here's where I need your help. I dated someone before I met my ex; he was running in the streets and got locked up. When he got out he looked for me, I felt terrible, and we started talking, and now we're together.

The problem is I don't like so many things about him. He keeps measly jobs; for months, when he got out, he didn't have a car, so he would drop me off at work and pick me up, using up all my gas. But I wanted him to have a chance, so I stuck it out. Now, he's better, but something is off. I don't know if I should stay and try to make things work, or be by myself or whatever. Signed, Divorced One in Maryland."

The air is quiet. The line is silent. Jameson uses this moment to his advantage to open the hearts of his audience—to receive their full attention. Plus he's getting his points together in his head.

"First of all, I want to commend you for even being on live radio on one of the most popular shows in the country. It takes courage to do that and especially to put yourself out there and your situation," Jameson charms the pants off of a panda.

"Thank you, I need your help," says the woman.

"There is a lot to unpack here. I'll touch on three areas... parents, standards and the impact on our culture. First, I want to talk about a theory I developed about parents. There are three types of parents out there in the world, in my humble opinion," being careful and stepping lightly, Jameson continues, "The first type are the men or women who literally never gave a damn about their children or took care of them.

Growing up, a lot of my friends referred to their fathers mainly as sperm donors because they never had a relationship with their offspring. We won't even get into those type of parents because they aren't worth discussing. So let's speak on the other two types of parents. You have C- parents and A- parents, Keisha."

"C- and A- parents, please explain further," Keisha pries.

Jameson eagerly continues...

"Back in college, there was a phrase that C's get degrees, and it's true. You can literally get all C's in most majors, not all but some, and walk across that stage. Very average, but you did it. Let's relate that to parenting, C parents check all the damn boxes. Their kids go to school, they feed them, they check their homework some nights, they mostly care that their kid passes school, they do just enough to have their kids graduate into adulthood. Now, on the surface and from a distance, you'll think things are good. The children seem happy, and so are the parents because they can be lazy by doing just enough and not have to put in real work. These children typically flounder around for years, not doing much or accomplishing anything because nobody ever pushed them to be great. All they had to get was average, and that was always acceptable.

But when you get up and really look at the situation of a C-parent, they're rejecting their child or children. It reeks of neglect because they are not molding or helping to guide their children in the right direction. They're letting them get by but just doing enough to not fail or really succeed, settling for being average.

A- parents, check the same boxes as C- parents, but they invest, reinvest and continue to deposit more and more into their children. These are parents that go to their children's boring baseball games, they listen to their long stories when they're 3- and 4-years-old, and don't really make sense but they sit there, intently and listen. They come home, tired but still play with their kids. They take time to make sure they look good when they go to school in the morning because they know their children are a reflection of them.

A- parents also put time in with their children daily. It could be something as simple as talking to your children each day, not just the standard *how was school* and *good,* but *what did you learn, tell me something new you learned in school*, and not letting simple one word answers suffice. They care to know their children's friends as they get older and want to hang out. They want to know their friends' parents as well. These are parents that get intertwined with their children's lives, and it's not to be nosey or be in their business, but it's to help guide them into adulthood. When a child is in their first 8, 9 years the most important thing you can show them is simple and free... love.

A- parents show love to their children all the time, C- parents to do it occasionally. A- parents kids know their parents love them, C- parents think their parents love and care for them, but they don't feel it in their soul.

Now young lady, your current boyfriend... does he have any children at all?"

"Yes, he does. He has three kids," the woman says.

"How often does he see his kids?"

"Every other weekend...."

"How often does your ex see your children?"

"We do one week on and one week off, he has them as much as I do," the woman responds.

"Now if I had to guess, I would think that you and your ex are both A- parents that I just spoke about?"

"Yes, we aren't perfect but I think we're both A- parents."

"What about your boyfriend?"

The woman pauses for a moment and responds quietly, "He's a C- parent unfortunately."

"And I don't want to downgrade C- parents, they get the job done, but if you're going to invest in anything, invest in your children. They didn't ask to be here so the least you can do is give them the best shot in life.... Anyway, getting into standards. I knew your boyfriend was a C- parent. But the standards I am speaking about are your standards."

"My standards?" repeats the woman.

"Yes, when you were married, outside of your ex cheating how did he treat you. And what I mean is, what kind of respect did he show you in front of your children?"

"He was a gentlemen, he opened doors for me, he opened my car door, he treated me like a lady. Now he still cheated...."

Jameson laughs, "I apologize for laughing but there is no excuse for him cheating but your standard in most situations was high, these were things you expected from him and came to expect, would you say that's true?"

"Yes."

"This is not a perfect analogy but stick with me everyone. We can't do anything about him cheating but see how this gets tricky. So, you had high standards on how you wanted to be treated as a woman, your ex cheated and instead of you keeping your standards high, you lowered them to find a man. A man that truthfully wouldn't have made the cut when you were younger but now you're with him, and you feel stuck."

"Yeah I do, completely stuck now."

Jameson continues, "Let's turn this on everyone listening. Woman, I'm going to be very blunt and this is not anything new but it's the first time I am saying it on this show. Men will only give you as much respect as you demand. And the trick is you have to have high standards from the beginning, you can't go back and try to make your standards high afterwards.

From the very beginning, if you let your man not open doors for you, not fill your car up with gas, not respect you enough to not call you a bitch and you respond, not have enough love for his own kids to see them, then how can you expect him to show you respect three years down the line? You already spoiled him, it's like giving a kid candy for dinner until they're 12 and on their 13th birthday now you want to implement broccoli and vegetables, it's too late now.

Your standard needs to be your own standard, whatever it is, stick with it and do not let down. If someone is below your standard, and you normally know quickly, just move the hell on. Otherwise you'll be five years in, and feel trapped because you sullied your relationship from the jump. Does this make any sense?" Jameson asks the woman on the line.

"It does, it makes total sense," she replies.

"I won't go too philosophical on the last point so I will keep it short. When women allow men to misuse and mistreat them, it creates a spiral effect," Jameson continues, "Your children rather they are boys or girls are watching, and watching a lot more than we give them credit for.

A young girl sees a man not treating her mother right, she'll think that's how she should be treated. A young man sees his mother's boyfriend not treating her well, he will follow in those footsteps. And from there it's a repetitive cycle, rinse and repeat, again and again.

Miss Divorced One in Maryland, I believe you know exactly what you should do. If you aren't happy, then you do not need to be in a relationship, not this one anyway. You have no need to feel afraid of being alone, savor those times, grow, learn from past mistakes and become wise enough not to repeat them."

"Yes I do, you're right. Without question you are right," says the woman in response.

"Dr. Black Love, we went over on time but that was very good. I think most of us can learn something from that today. Miss Divorced One in Maryland, we will get back to you in a few weeks for an update. Dr. Black Love, take us home please," Keisha says.

"Great show tonight. Until tomorrow remember... love only enters if the heart is willing, signing off, Dr. Black Love."

37

Family Time

Jameson pulls up to his childhood home and parks in the back. He spent many days running around the playground, swinging on the swings, and running through the sprinklers. He can still imagine himself running on the top court at Ozanam's basketball summer leagues as a teenager.

Great memories of his childhood, many nights spent just looking up at the stars discussing who is the best rapper of that time or what kind of car they would have as adults.

Unfortunately, most of his friends from those times are no longer around; they became statistics, caught up in the system, or rarely thought of or all-out disappeared. *So many black men become nothing in this country,* he thought to himself. He felt blessed, lucky, and guilty about his success, yet so many others never even made it into their late 20's.

He comes back to reality and realizes that Ryann and Zanita are with him, and he feels good. As a young man, he would often daydream about having a big family, coming back home to see his loving parents with three or four kids, a wife, a dog, the whole nine. But reality doesn't always run the same path as our daydreams. So here he was with his only child in the back seat, his high school sweetheart in the front seat, his ex-wife 2,000 miles away, his parents are just speaking after taking an extended hiatus. Jameson thinks to himself and laughs, "Damn, life loves to give you a big middle finger sometimes."

All things considered, he was in a good place. Less than a year from moving back home, the foundation for the future is solidifying. The two lovely ladies in the vehicle with him are a big part of it. Zanita is doing exceptionally well in school and has adjusted fairly well to the colder temperatures of the east coast. Ryann, in his eyes, is perfect; she is supportive when needed, knows when to back off, is a great mother figure to Zanita; he could not ask for someone better by his side.

Tonight was important; it was sort of a re-establishment of the Clarkson family. After many years of distance and turmoil, there is a new normal shaping form. The only person missing was his brother, but that would have to be tackled another day.

"Ladies, let's get inside."

Everyone exits the vehicle and walks inside the house.

Zanita hugs her grandparents, Jameson embraces his parents, Ryann is re-introduced to Mr. and Mrs. Clarkson. As expected, Mr. Clarkson hugs Ryann a little too long, but the moment passes. Finally, they all take a seat in the living room before dinner.

"Thank you so much for inviting us over," Ryann says.

"We appreciate you coming Ryann," Mr. Clarkson replies.

Mrs. Clarkson stares at her husband and raises her eyebrows in a warning signal.

Mr. Clarkson catches a glimpse and stutters, "Of course, we appreciate everyone coming. Do you all want anything to drink?"

"No, we're good Dad. What's for dinner?" Jameson chuckles.

"I baked a chicken, made some vegetables with it, sweet potatoes."

"That sounds so damn good...." Jameson stops himself, "Sorry for the language, Mom."

"Can we eat?" asks Zanita.

"We will Z, in a few minutes," Jameson reassures his anxious little girl.

"Ryann, what do you do for a living? It's been so long since we've seen you," Mrs. Clarkson turns to face Ryann.

"I run a non-profit downtown that focuses on helping young women of color get jobs in fortune 500 companies."

"That's impressive," Mr. Clarkson chimes in.

Jameson scratches the back of his head from the looks his mother is giving his father.

"She's amazing at it, she's the Founder and Executive Director, she started and runs the entire organization," Jameson says.

"It's not a top evening radio show but we're doing things as well," Ryann replies, winking at Jameson.

"I get paid to talk, and for some reason people like it."

"Well that mouth of yours has always been good and bad for you," Mrs. Clarkson says.

"How so Mom?"

"Ever since you could talk, you've always had a lot to say, you're very smart but you can speak before you think sometimes. I heard about your suspension," Mrs. Clarkson now gives Jameson the same raised eyebrow.

Jameson looks at his dad and shakes his head in disappointment, and smiles.

"What you want me to do, she asked so I couldn't lie to her," Jameson says in his defense.

"We can't have conversations in confidence without you running off and telling mom now," Jameson says as everyone laughs.

"You know I can't listen to all that crazy talk Jameson but my girlfriends at church listen."

"Really, what do they say?" Jameson asks.

"They say you're very good with advice, they just hope you listen to your own advice."

"I think he is now, Mrs. Clarkson, I had to straighten him up a little of course," Ryann says.

"Well good, I always liked you. Just had to wait for him to catch up that's all."

"I'm caught up now mother," Jameson says, smiling.

"Zanita, what do you think of your dad's girlfriend?" Mr. Clarkson asks.

Zanita looks a little confused, "Daddy doesn't have a girlfriend, Ryann is his friend."

"Oh, I see. What do you think about Ryann, Daddy's friend?" Mr. Clarkson asks.

"She's very nice and pretty, I like her. If Daddy did have a girlfriend it should be somebody like Ryann."

"Children are very smart, very smart indeed," Mr. Clarkson says in reply.

"Mom, is it time to eat?" Jameson interrupts.

"Yes, let's sit down at the table," Mrs. Clarkson replies.

At the dinner table, everyone is seated, the food is served.

Mr. Clarkson stands up, "Everyone please bow your heads and hold hands."

Mr. Clarkson grabs Ryann's hand to the left and holds Zanita's hand to the right. Jameson smiles at Ryann and closes his eyes.

"Dear Lord, we thank you for this evening. This evening of fellowship and family. Please bless the hands that prepared this food, and please protect us on the highways and byways as everyone returns home. In Jesus name we pray, Amen."

Everyone repeats Amen.

"Everyone, let's eat," Mrs. Clarkson says and begins making plates for her two favorite men.

38

Kolby's Birthday

In a typical year, Kolby has a huge birthday bash down at his lounge. He enjoys the time inviting people who have moved away, inviting anyone in the city, and having a good time celebrating another year on earth. This year, however, is totally different. The gathering is at Kolby's home, very low key, especially considering Kolby's typical celebrations. There are not more than 20 people total at the house.

Bottles are still being popped, and a considerable amount of drinking is taking place, especially by the evening host. Kolby does not miss three things very often: a beautiful woman, a chance to drink, and an opportunity to talk shit. Tonight, he is in his element and will not dare miss a chance to get two out of the three.

As the night dies down, Kolby, Eero, and Jameson are shooting pool as they typically do.

"I'm telling you right now, I'll put any amount of money and argue with anyone that Lebron Raymone James, Sr. is the best player to ever lace up sneakers, period. He's the King for a reason," Kolby shouts before he takes another shot.

"Oh my... here we go with this shit," Jameson responds.

Kolby takes another drink of henny and coke before continuing, "He has been the best player in the league for like 10, 12 years. MJ didn't do that, Kobe didn't do that, Magic didn't do that, Kareem didn't do that. He's been the best longer, so that makes him the greatest."

"Lebron is a freak of nature bro. This dude is 6'9, 260 pounds, with guard skills. He's as big as Karl Malone but is like a point guard. So of course he's going to last longer than Mike. Mike was like 190 pounds when he left Carolina," Jameson explains.

"So you using his God-given size against him, nobody else that big and strong has done what Lebron, the King has done. That makes him even greater to me. We've seen a carbon copy of MJ, and that was Kobe. God rest his soul. We've never seen anyone like Lebron and we won't ever again," Kolby states bluntly.

"6 and 0, simple as that. MJ never lost in the chip, he would bust LBJ's ass if they played during the same generation," Jameson belts back.

"No he wouldn't," Eero chips in.

"What!?" Jameson says, not believing his ears.

"I'm not saying MJ isn't better but people act like LBJ is not one of the greatest ever. You can go back and forth about who might be better and both have valid points. We can never have these discussions and elevate both of them, it has to be one over the other and you put the other one down. We need to stop that, just enjoy them both for their greatness."

Jameson and Kolby both look at Eero sideways.

"What the fuck ever Eero, this is what we do," Kolby says.

"Go somewhere with that politically correct mumble nonsense," Jameson adds.

"Y'all two just keep going on and on about this shit and there is no winner," Eero says.

"I always win debates with both of you, period. Jameson Clarkson does not lose debates or arguments very often, unless it's answering to my 5-year-old daughter. I can't win shit with her," Jameson says proudly.

They all bust out laughing.

"All jokes aside, I'll tell you why people hate Lebron so much," Kolby starts again.

"Please bless us with this lesson the omniscient one," Jameson says jokingly, but Kolby ignores him and keeps talking.

"Let's look at Mike... he was one of the most protected athletes ever. Nike marketed him, be like Mike; he was so pristine to people. But that's because there was no internet, there was no 24/7 press outside of ESPN, maybe. Everyone wasn't looking for a story to break. So Mike was put on a pedestal nobody had even been close to until Tiger came along. And we saw how far his ass fell because of media, thirsty ass media outlets, and shit like that.

Mike was basically a perfect athlete for white America. He didn't ruffle any feathers, not publicly at least. He played ball, did his commercials, and most importantly, stayed quiet. He lived in Chicago, with all the violence going on then and still to this day, but did nothing publicly. He never went after anyone politically that was wrong; he never did any of that. He just sold his Jordan's, kept making millions, and again, shut the hell up publicly.

Now here comes Lebron; he's from a single mother, he brings his people with him, gives them a platform and allows them to shine as well, speaks his mind about whatever he damn well pleases. He brought his childhood friends along and said we are going to build this together. And look at them now... they out here killing the game in all types of shit. So you got brothas that make it and build a house, try to sit on all the money and forget about their people.

Now, he is the opposite of Mike in a lot of ways; he uses the things he is given for his agenda, not the other way around.

Even Space Jam, you know he had Spike Lee's cousin direct that, a white man directed the one Mike did. That's not a coincidence, and he does it publicly; he stood up for Travon Martin; he stood up for black people being assassinated by these racists ass police out here in these streets. He builds a school back in his hometown to help kids like him be successful; he puts time, money, and effort into causes that help our people.

So why is Lebron hated... because they can't control him. Now he's tactical at what he goes after, but he is definitely not scared to lose money, and he doesn't. People are mad cause he said, I'm taking my talents to South Beach. If that's all you gotta say about him, then he's done a fucking great job at being a husband, father, basketball player, and role model. Far better than Mike ever did, period. And if for nothing else, that's why he's number one on my list."

Both Eero and Jameson take in what was just said.

"You know what, everything you said was right. I can't take none of that away from Lebron. American's worst nightmare, young, rich and not scared. He's exceeded expectations which is incredible... But he still ain't better than Mike on the court to me, don't matter what you say."

Kolby waves him, and they start playing pool again.

"Isn't that the problem with our people though, I mean people in general but us as black people. We hate on success of our own so much." Says Eero.

"Without question, we can be our own worst enemy. Take the lounge for instance, we get knuckleheads that come in starting shit, causing issues with the kitchen; if we was a white establishment that would never happen. That's some sucker shit there, you cause issues with your own but walk with a tail between your legs in front of white people. That pisses me off so much," Kolby says.

"And it seems to only be us, black people. Like I don't see Asians going into an Asian business and causing issues. Or any other races doing that really besides us," Eero agrees.

"That goes back to how we got here, we've always just been put against each other. Light skin versus dark skinned, house versus field negroes, it's hard as hell to break that cycle when it happened for so long. We need to rise above it and stop, period," Jameson says outrightly.

"I don't think it'll happen, I hate to say it. We have no leaders besides athletes and Al Sharpton is getting old," Jameson says.

They all start laughing.

"Seriously though," Jameson continues. "Like whose next in line, that makes me nervous. When something goes down, Sharpton is there. We need the next Sharpton or Sharptons to be ready. And now while the man is still here, give him his roses and prepare the next generation.

You know the simple answer fellas… love. We just don't love each other enough. If we did, most of our issues wouldn't even be issues. Whatever happened to us in the past, we need to learn from it and it will help change the present and future. We do it in our individual homes, with our children and our families, but it doesn't spread like it should."

"Y'all two trying to ruin my birthday with all this deep shit," Kolby says.

"You the one giving dissertations on Lebron James a few minutes ago," Jameson says in response.

"I needed to school you so I had to go deep. I can do that from time to time Dr. Black Love, you ain't the only one with knowledge."

"Take your drunk ass to sleep."

"Not before I beat you again in another round. Corner pocket," Kolby hits the shot, "Rack 'em Jameson."

39

Much Needed Talk

ameson is at the top of the stairs leading down to his dad's den. He can't help but notice how both his parents seem happier now. They are interacting and spending time with one another. It's been a beautiful transformation from when he first stepped foot in the house several months ago. However, there is one piece of their family that is still missing... Larry.

Lawrence "Larry" Clarkson is Jameson's elder brother by four years. Growing up, he was Jameson's idol. He was older, wiser, bigger, and more robust, and Jameson felt that his brother could do anything. They had a good relationship; Larry never left his brother behind and made him feel irrelevant.

Jameson would even be permitted to hang out with some of Larry's older friends from time to time. That all changed in a blink of an eye, on one fateful night over 20 years ago.

Larry was a Senior in high school when he went to a party. He was not much for drinking or anything, but that night he drank and smoked. Unfortunately, whatever he smoked that night was not what he thought it was. He started hallucinating and acting out of his mind; so bad, in fact, he was left on their back door by some of his friends as he had nearly passed out at the party.

Larry woke up and was still not himself; he was outside of the house and, for some reason, started a fire. The details get a bit murky to Jameson after this point, but Larry ended up being arrested; he was never charged, but Mr. Clarkson banned him from ever entering their home again, and he never spoke to him again to this day.

Larry eventually moved away, bounced around here and there, and even occasionally, Jameson would lose touch with him. Jameson knew he would contact Mrs. Clarkson, but his name was never mentioned again in their home. Jameson missed his brother; he felt in his heart that everyone else did as well. For all the things Jameson loved about his father, this one was a subject that caused him much consternation. On the one hand, he understood why his father was so upset; if Larry had successfully set their entire home on fire, their home could have burned down, or even worse, someone lost their life.

On the other hand, he also felt that his father was unreasonable as Larry was not in his right mind that night. He tried to smoke weed; he was not a bad kid; he made a mistake. He felt the time was right to speak to his dad about Larry. Jameson made his way down the steps.

"Dad, how you doing?" Jameson asks.

"Doing good son, I'm just down here relaxing. Nothing is wrong with me and your mother."

"Yeah I know, she's upstairs singing so I know she's good." Jameson takes a seat.

"Where is my beautiful granddaughter?"

"She's with the nanny, she just got out of school. So I stopped by before I headed down to the studio for the show tonight. I don't have a lot of time but we need to talk."

"What's on your mind?"

"I don't really know how to start this conversation... Dad, I think we should try to have some type of relationship with Larry."

Mr. Clarkson responds coldly, "No."

"Why not?"

"That fool tried to kill us, if it was anyone else they would be in jail right now probably still for trying to harm our family."

"You know that wasn't Larry that night. He wasn't a bad person, he just made a mistake," Jameson pleads his brother's case.

"A mistake is staying out too late or being in a stolen car or something stupid like that. Your brother tried to burn down our home, with us in it. I don't care what kind of laced weed he had, if you can do that once, you can do it again."

Jameson covers his face with his hands; the years of frustration and angst over this particular subject always impact him physically. The pain of not having a relationship makes him feel guilty; he sided with his father and never really checked in with Larry. He allowed someone else to dictate his relationship or lack thereof, and the 20+ years were now eating at him too much. "Dad, I love you. I think you're one of the best men I have ever met. You always taught me family is first and I get that Larry did something really foul and stupid. But it's been over 20 years and we still haven't moved an inch to try to bring our family back together. I think its time do that, it's been way too long," Jameson stands up; his dad is looking out the window.

"Pride is a form of selfishness... growing up, you used to make us remember all these quotes. You said it would help us later in life, well here is one I didn't understand when I was a kid but now I do. Here's Larry's number, call him Dad, talk to your son."

Jameson places a card on the table and walks out.

40

Showtime (Part 5)

"Dr. Black Love, we have a letter today from a white female," Keisha explains.

"That's good, I love it. We do not get many letters from different ethnicities to this point but I appreciate it," Jameson says in response.

"I think this could be another topic that will be discussed in our after hours show which I host every night. Gotta give the after party show some love," Keisha slides in.

"No question, thank you all for showing Keisha love on that. Live on Instagram about 15 minutes after our show ends. And you have been doing an amazing job with that segment, I must say. I'm on there for a bit, but I have to get home to baby girl...."

"We know, this is for the single people with no responsibilities, I'll hold it down for us both," Keisha teases.

They all laugh.

"Very much appreciated, I do hop on there, occasionally."

"Yeah, yeah we know you have blessed us with your presence every now and then. But anyway, let's get on with this letter and your response," Keisha reads...

"Dear Dr. Black Love, I love your show, and I have told everyone to watch, listen and I hope you have continued success. I am a white female, in my thirties, with two mixed children. For most of my life, I have been attracted to black men and nothing else really. However, recently I have started to at least explore dating men of other ethnicities. And I had a surprising interaction with one particular white male.

Long story short, we went out at dinner, and yes, we met on one of those dating apps. We started talking about our children, and I told him I have two kids with a Black father. His entire demeanor changed, he asked questions about my past, and I damn near thought I was being interrogated. I eventually got up and left, but I wondered what the hell was that about. I will never change who I am or what I love. But I would like some understanding on it, can you help me? Signed, Ms. Slightly confused," Keisha looks up at Jameson and smiles.

Jameson sits there and is silent for a moment. Then, he begins to play with his beard and rub his head.

"I have a feeling this is one of those types of letters," Keisha says, sensing Jameson's energy.

"I will say this, for me to truly answer this question I am going to piss some people off. I will say this, if you get pissed off that means I am probably talking about you... I will repeat, if you get pissed off, I am probably talking about you. Hell I feel like a preacher here...." Jameson states his disclaimer.

"Well... preach on sir," Keisha chimes in.

"Stop it, stop it. You will have my mother calling me tonight," Jameson says.

They both laugh.

"Here is the very simple answer to your question Miss Slightly Confused... In this country, as a backdrop there has always been a fear of the black penis," Jameson says.

"Oh lawd, here we go," Keisha says, rolling her eyes.

"Now, not everyone has this complex or fear even. Let's look at stereotypes of black men. We have all heard them, and to a certain degree, black men even accept the ones that make us seem better than most. But look on the flip side, you have some white men, not all, but some, that hate black men because of it.

They hate black athletes; you have noticed that when a black athlete leaves for free agency, he is typically vilified way more than when a white athlete does the same. In the arena or field, the boos are way louder and more pronounced.

Let's take it to the 'real world', there will be white men that will never date anyone who has ever slept with a black man; it's like they're tainted. In this situation, that white man would never continue to pursue this young lady. Instead, he looks down on her like she is less than because she has two children with a black man.

This goes back to when we first got here. The stereotype of us being bigger, stronger, faster, more well-endowed pissed off those slave owners. So what did they do? They raped our women, beat black men, separated our families, castrated black men—all because of hatred and the need for power.

So, Miss Slight Confused, if you continue to date men, and this isn't even just for white men only, you will find more of this in other ethnicities and races as well. Black men in this country are hated on all over the world, and unfortunately, that will probably always be the case," Jameson says matter of factly, proud that he spoke his truth, and from a place of his truth.

"Way to lay it on 'em thick tonight sir," Keisha chimes in.

"I am here to help educate and entertain. Great job tonight, Keisha."

"Yes, same to you as well. We appreciate you all listening and we will be back tomorrow. Sign us off, Dr. Black Love."

"Please remember... love only enters if the heart is willing, signing off, Dr. Black Love," Jameson says with a little more oomph than any other time, as if he is awaiting the call from the powers that be upstairs.

"We definitely will hear from people about that last topic," Keisha says to Jameson.

"Abraham, what you think?" Jameson asks.

Abraham walks into the studio, "It's the truth bro, you always speak from a place of truth." Abraham shrugs his shoulders and walks back out.

Jameson is packing his backpack in anticipation of leaving.

"Jameson, you got a minute?" Keisha asks.

"What's up."

"You always run up out of here before we get much chance to just talk. And I know why, but how are things with you?"

Jameson stops packing his bag and ponders how to answer.

"Keisha, my life is good. I moved here to start all over, and I was scared as hell truthfully. I know I front like I got all my shit together, but I didn't know if this would work, moving home was always a dream but it was way out there in the clouds for real."

"That's interesting, you didn't seem nervous at all when I met you," she says.

"I can't show that, hell if I show I'm nervous then what would you be... I needed you to be you, that's why I chose you. Well, we did, but technically it was me."

"Fake it til you make it."

"Right, but like most things we have to project strength, underneath it all I was nervous. Now they can't tell me shit. I have my baby girl here, the rest of my family, my girl, my people. I can do it all now, life is beautiful."

"I can tell you're happy, you have a little glow about you. Your demeanor is different, you're still you, but you're more at ease. It's nice to see."

"I am glad you notice, that's definitely a good thing."

"Good talking with you, I'm gonna get prepped for the after show."

"Kill it like you always do."

Keisha walks out of the studio. Jameson waves to Abraham to come into the studio. "Abraham, have I ever offended you on the show?"

"No, I may not totally get your perspective but I've never been offended."

"What have you been then?"

"Good question... I have laughed, been enlightened, encouraged, saddened, all those things and more by you. You're quite a unique person, I appreciate working with you."

"Thank you."

"Why did you ask me that?" Abraham asks curiously.

"I know we don't kick it after work but I respect you and I don't want to hurt you from the perspective of being ignorant or offensive. I have learned from your perspective on things and I just wanted to check."

"Appreciated."

"I need to get out of here, have a good evening," Jameson grabs his bag.

They give each other dap, and Jameson leaves.

Jameson checks his phone and sees several missed calls from Eero; he calls back.

"What up, why you calling me during the show. You know I can't answer."

"Y'all need to come to my office right now," Eero says.

"What the fuck Eero, come on...."

"No, I'm serious. Can't even discuss on the phone. Just come be here in ten." Eero hangs up.

Jameson stops walking; he is puzzled.

He texts his nanny that he'll be about an hour late, then heads out to Eero's office.

4

Shit Is Real

*J*ameson walks into Eero's office; Eero and Kolby are already seated. But, unfortunately, the vibe in the office was very thick; the usual harmonious vibe that was always present between the three of them was met with dissonance... something was off, and Jameson could sense it immediately. Eero looked as if he had not slept in a week, and Kolby had a look that he wanted to rip someone's head off.

"What's wrong?" Jameson asks.

"You should take a seat for this one," Kolby says pointing at the empty chair in front of Eero's desk.

Jameson walks and sits, raising his hands and eyebrows in anticipation of the news.

"Eero... tell him, this is your story to break."

"I found out a few months ago there could be an excavation project on the 2200 block of Webster Avenue. I didn't say anything because I didn't know if it would happen. Now I know it will, and it'll happen soon."

"How *soon* is soon?" Jameson asks Eero.

"Within the next couple weeks soon," Eero replies.

Jameson looks kind of confused, "When I moved, the last thing we talked about was making sure this shit was taken care of. We all talked about it, as a matter of fact, Kolby, you assured me that we would be good. What the fuck happened to that?"

"It don't really matter, it never got taken care of. I just didn't get it taken care of," Kolby responds.

"You knew this Eero?"

Eero nods in acknowledgment.

Jameson is pissed and hurt. Not only did he feel betrayed, but he also felt that he had been lied to deliberately by the two people closest to him. Jameson puts his face inside his hands and breathes deeply. "Damn, I don't even know what to say to either of you. We knew there was one thing that no matter what we do, could fuck everything up that we've built.

Eero, you are an elected official, you work for the public. If this shit comes out, that is over. Kolby, none of your businesses run if you aren't there. This is just sloppy as hell, and I guess y'all want me to figure it out," Jameson is annoyed as hell.

"We didn't ask you to figure out anything, we needed for you to know. So we can *all* figure it out," Eero replies, "You ain't Captain America for us, we don't need you to save the day, we just need to put our heads together and come up with a plan."

"Truthfully, ever since you left, it's just been different. You fucked up the trio bro," Kolby spits out bitterly.

"So now, you're blaming me for you basically lying to us and not handling everything?" Jameson replies. "Maaaaaannn..."

"No, I always take responsibility for my shit. Like I said, you left and things just changed. And it just slipped my mind, that's it," Kolby offers an explanation.

"That's a lame ass excuse, I'm just disappointed and surprised at you Kolby. I don't get it."

"It didn't get done, you didn't ask either Jameson. Let's just end it there," Eero interjects.

"It would've been easier if you told us when you found out, that way it could've been taken care of already," Kolby says to Eero.

"I really didn't know what to do...."

"So you chose to do nothing, that's literally the worse option you could have chosen. Even if you told one of us, we'd be in a better spot now," Jameson replies.

"You want me to apologize, what good would that do? It won't change a damn thing anyway. So what's the point? Let's not forget, Kolby, this was supposed to be handled by you like ten years ago."

"I got a lot of shit to handle on a daily basis. Eventually that just slipped my mind, but that was unintentional, Eero. Yo' ass literally just said *fuck it I won't tell 'em*. That makes no damn sense at all," Kolby rebuttal.

"You're not gonna keep blaming me for this. This all goes back to you and your quick temper, Kolby. Ever since we was kids, you always got us into shit, we got us out, but YOU was the catalyst for most of the negative shit that came up!" Eero replies.

"We had to keep your scary ass in line, you couldn't hold your own when we was young, Eero."

"Enough! Enough of the petty shit. Kolby, we know you got a temper. Eero, we know you can be sensitive. Me, I'm just an asshole. Let's put it on the table, who cares?" Jameson interjects.

There is an uneasy silence.

Even in the best relationships, there are always seeds of contempt, jealousy, or spite built up. Quite often, they are brushed under the rug and never properly dealt with. They come out in situations where someone is hurt, angry, or both. Words are spewed, which can hurt a relationship for a season or lifetime.

Not that they are not valid, but because a loved one would have the audacity to mention a flaw about another loved one. We can retreat to corners or argue them out, but quite often, it changes that relationship forever once the damage is done.

The three brothers had never faced an adversary between themselves, and cracks in their friendship have become apparent when facing the uncharted territory. The only way to recover from this was to have a genuine conversation, leaving no card unturned and making yourself vulnerable—the exact opposite of what these three had worked towards their entire lives.

You could not expose yourself growing up in their neighborhood, being from their block, or even in their homes. To save themselves and each other, they had to show their cards or face the music on their own.

"Crazy Eddie was my Uncle," Kolby says.

Both Eero and Jameson quickly look at Kolby, startled.

"I never trusted anyone besides my mother and you two. That's why I told you, I always felt as a crew, we could do anything. I knew if we put our minds to it, we would take care of it, and it would be over. You two the only fools I ever trusted, and that's still true to this day," Kolby says.

"I apologize to you both, this all caught me off guard...." Jameson says.

"I screwed this up, I just wanted to figure it out myself. Instead, I put us in a worse position," Eero chimes in.

"What if we do nothing?" Jameson says. "They find a body, they find a body. Crazy Eddie don't have any kin that are looking for him. It can be a story, but it dies within a week tops."

"That could work...." Eero says.

Kolby shakes his head in disagreement, "No, no it won't. That asshole grabbed my chain," Kolby says, "The chain that my grandmother, his sister, gave to all of my cousins. It has my name and birthdate on it."

"Fuck..." Jameson says again places his face in his hands.

Again, there is an awkward length of silence between the three of them.

"We only have one real solution," Jameson says.

"What's that?" Eero asks.

"We go get the body tonight. We meet, come up with a game plan and dig that shit up ourselves. That way nobody else knows still."

"What we gonna do with whatever is left?" Eero asks.

"I'll figure that out, let's get the first part done and go from there. Let's meet here in an hour," Jameson says standing up.

They give each other dap and leave.

As Jameson leaves, he can feel the uneasiness of the situation taking over his body. He felt nauseous, fatigued, and nervous all at the same time. He had been on such a high lately, and now that was all tumbling down. As he said earlier today though he had to push through it, he could not show any weakness to Eero or Kolby. That would break the group's confidence down, and he needed everyone to be on point tonight in all their actions.

Jameson picked up his phone to text Ryann.

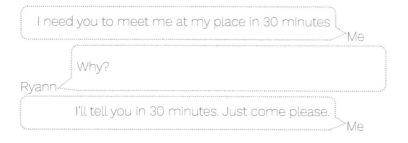

I need you to meet me at my place in 30 minutes
Me

Why?
Ryann

I'll tell you in 30 minutes. Just come please.
Me

Jameson continued out the building and into the ever growing dark skies of downtown.

42

Trust Me

*J*ameson paces back and forth; he can't sit. His drink for tonight carries his namesake Jameson on the rocks—typically pulled out for holidays or special occasions, which tonight classifies.

He is dressed in all black from head to toe, as agreed upon, like something from the movies. He stops and looks outside; tonight is kind of dreary, a little cooler than it's been recent. To him, it fits the mood of the evening since he stepped into Eero's office.

Riding waves of emotion is part of life, and as he grew up, he realized that with a high always comes a low. So to prepare for the eventual low, he was always laser-focused on hitting the next high, which worked for him in his younger years. It allowed him to bounce from relationship to relationship, both professionally and romantically and not give too much of himself.

The old saying, you meet someone for a reason, season, or lifetime applied to him perfectly. The only lifetime friends he had were back home; everyone else was damn near a castaway on his evolution in his lifetime.

He was never crass, disingenuous, or rude, but he never gave his all to anyone. Not out of ignorance but fear, fear that if he gave his all, it would end and he would be hurt; fear that if you love someone, they will leave eventually anyway; fear that if you allow someone in, it never has a happy ending.

Since Zanita was born, he has graduated to higher levels of thinking. Seeing her for the first time, he knew he had to enjoy every single moment. He had to give all he had to her and other people, he had a duty and responsibility as a man, father, and human being to continue moving things forward. Being selfish and only taking would no longer be acceptable to him. Since moving back home, reuniting with his brothers, his family, and other friends, and Ryann, he has enjoyed each day even more so.

Tonight brings up old wounds from the past and reminds him of why he chose to move and not leave any remnants behind. Nobody can outrun their past forever, and this is their time to deal with something so painful that even as a grown man, it brings uneasiness and anxiety that he has not felt since that night over twenty years ago.

The door opens, Jameson turns, and Ryann walks in.

"Hey," Jameson says as he walks over and hugs her and kiss. "Thank you for coming over."

"I can always help you but why the rush?" Ryann asks.

"Let's take a seat," Jameson leads her to the dining room table, she sits while Jameson checks on Zanita. Sound asleep like the beautiful princess she is... Jameson closes the door to her room and joins Ryann at the dining room table. Jameson pours more whiskey.

"I see you're drinking for yourself tonight."

Jameson shrugs, "If you only knew...."

"So tell me, what the hell is going on?"

"Do you trust me?"

"Jameson, are we going to go through five minutes of me begging you?"

"I really need you to answer me, without asking questions, this is serious shit." Jameson stares back, without blinking and his deliberate nature sheds some light to Ryann that this isn't a normal conversation.

"Yes, I think I trust you more than I ever have," Ryann says, starting to feel a little nervous and uneasy.

"I have only trusted four or five people for basically my entire life. My parents, and mainly my father, my mother is my mother but I know how she is... Eero and Kolby. Ever since Larry left, that cut off everyone else from getting that close to me. When we first met and got older, I began to feel myself letting you in, that's one of the reasons I left. I never want to be vulnerable with anyone, it gives too much power to another person," Jameson drinks again and looks away.

He continues, "When I moved back here, I was focused on the show and getting ready for Z to move here, that's it. Two purposes, and if I perfected those, everything would fall into place. Then I see you, looking and smelling even better than you did ten years ago or so...."

They both smile at each other.

"Sometimes I feel like a fraud on my show, I tell people all the time to let love in but I never have. I can give the best advice but can't follow it. Because of fear I never allow myself to follow it...."

"So you rushed me over here, in the cold for true confessions of Jameson Clarkson," Ryann says, smiling.

"No, no. I just needed to give some context to what I am about to say. I know that you allowed me to see how amazing you are now and always have been. You allowed me to jump off the cliff of love and not look back or even more importantly be fearful. I am grateful for that, thank you."

"You're welcome."

"Tonight, I need you to do the same for me, at least for now."

"What do you mean?"

"That same faith, that same fearlessness that I have come to accept and immerse myself in, I need you to give me that same grace, right now."

"What did you do?"

"If you listen to me, and if I make it back, I will tell you everything. I can't tell you before though."

Ryann is uncomfortable with the answer.

"This goes 100% against your go get 'em, type A personality, must know everything DNA. But you have to trust me, I'm protecting you by not telling you," Jameson pleads.

Ryann ponders for a moment.

"So, what if you don't make it back, since you said *if*?"

Jameson closes his eyes for a moment, opens them as he turns to Zanita's room and goes back to Ryann, and closes his eyes again. The gravity of that question hit home hard. But the task at hand was necessary and too great to back out now; he had to do it for his brothers.

Ryann does not wait for a response and walks to the other side of the table, grabs Jameson, and holds him close to her. "Just handle your business and get back here. I love you."

"I love you too."

Jameson checks the time and gets up.

"If Z wakes up, just tell her I had to run out. I need to leave."

They kiss quickly, and Jameson walks out.

43

Game Time

Themselves—

*T*he brothers knew cell phone communication was not an option. So they set up everything in Eero's office and had to follow it perfectly for their plan to be executed flawlessly.

Eero was always the one to come up with plans, even as children. If they planned to sneak out of the house in high school, if there was a plan needed to pull money together for a spring break trip, even down to figuring out how to eat out on a $2 a week budget in high school, Eero was the one expected to come up with the plan they could execute.

Tonight was no different, but the stakes are much higher than meeting your girlfriend to cop a kiss or go to some party on the other side of town, this is a plan needed to ensure the brothers' freedom, and flawless execution is a must.

Eero sits for a few moments alone, and there is not much conversation. The air is thick in the room, the sunlight of the day evaporates, and the gloominess of the evening creeps into the room. The sounds of men and women hustling to get home ceased, the sounds of buses zooming by died down, now there is an eerily quietness to downtown.

Kolby mindlessly scrolls through Instagram, not looking at anything in particular but to keep his mind preoccupied. Jameson sits with his face in his hands, attempting to fight the nauseous feeling that kept rising from his stomach. Neither Kolby nor Jameson spoke; they just sat and waited for Eero's plan.

Eero sits up and looks at them both, "Let's go over the plan. We can't use cell phones at all, when you get in the car, make sure it shows the real time. Once you get home, leave your phone on, but do not bring it." Kolby and Jameson both nod.

"I'm dead ass serious, if something happens later, they can track us with our phones. We're going to meet on the block at 10 p.m., on the nose. Jameson park on the 2100 block of Webster Avenue facing downtown and walk over. I'll park on 2200 block of Bedford Avenue and do the same. Kolby, park across the street since you have everything we need.

Wear all black, bring shovels, gloves, masks and flashlights. Give yourself enough time to meet at 10 p.m. when you park, don't get there early and look suspicious. See everyone this evening." They give each other dap, and they all leave.

Jameson went over his checklist; cell phone back home, all black, gloves, flashlight, and snow goggles. It was 9:56 p.m., the street was dark with few lights. As kids, they would run up and down these streets—whether it was by foot or bike—until the street lights came on and everyone would scatter home. Even as an adult, he would avoid driving on this particular block not to have to deal with his memories. Now he had to meet them head-on, ready or not.

Jameson and Eero arrive a couple of minutes before 10 p.m.; they give each other dap.

"I love being back in the neighborhood but not for this," Jameson says to Eero.

"I never drive down this way, I haven't in years," Eero says almost spooked out.

"You ever think about moving back?" Jameson asks.

"Back here... no, not really. I work right down the street, I come through all the time, but I don't think Mary would move back anyway."

"I feel like our kids miss a little edge not growing up like we did."

"That was the first thing we said we would not do is have our kids grow up like us. But I hear you, it's like a small piece of you wants them to understand the struggle."

"Right, so they can see how good they have it. I worry about our kids not knowing our culture as much, how to operate in all walks of life like we do," Jameson says.

"I guess it's just something we have to teach and show them, but truthfully it's a blessing to be able to say we have options for our children."

"True, very true."

"Here goes Kolby," Eero says, pointing across the street.

Kolby slowly pulls up in his Yukon. They both walk across the street to the window. Kolby rolls down his window, and they see Big Ray sitting in the passenger seat. Eero motions to say something, but Jameson grabs his hand holding him back. No time for disagreements or distractions right now.

Kolby starts, "Shovels are in the back seat, we have bags as well. After we dig up the body, Ray will sink it in one of the rivers, then that'll be it."

Everyone nods in agreement, and the three of them get out, grab what they need, and walk back across the street.

"Why you bring Ray, the less people that know the better?" Eero snorts at Kolby.

"I told you don't worry about nothing outside of what I tell you," Kolby responds without looking.

"At least tell us the plan afterwards," Jameson replies.

"Ray will sit there and watch out. After we're done he, drives my truck, sinks the body. We get rid of these clothes, Eero you go home, Jameson and I will head to Kolby's, and chill for a minute like nothing happened. Ray stops by the lounge, his car is there and we all leave eventually. That's it, simple."

They continue across the street and go on the side of an abandoned building.

"It was ten steps forward and five to the right, I remember it like it was yesterday." Jameson says. The brothers walk off the steps and begin to dig.

Ray, like most of Kolby's family, is a big guy. He's 6'5 and tips the scales at 250 pounds or so. He also enjoys the finest of cannabis regularly. So sitting as a lookout on a dark side street is not too thrilling of an assignment. He has a blunt, so he smokes it and relaxes, and eventually goes in and out of dozing off while sitting in the driver's seat.

The area is mostly deserted, which is why that area was chosen years ago, but not totally. There is always the chance of someone stumbling upon their conquest by simply walking their dog or veering through the area for no apparent reason or, as it is very prevalent in their childhood neighborhood, the ever lingering presence of the neighborhood eye-witness.

In the 90s, cities would develop programs that encouraged citizens to talk about illegal activities and tied them to financial rewards to deter crime in these neighborhoods. To most in the neighborhood, singing or snitching to authorities was not looked upon in positive light. The participants are typically older individuals that have retired but still get along pretty well. They feel it is their duty to make sure things around them operate normally, and if not, they will be quick to pick up the phone and call Pittsburgh's finest. Just about every block has one, and the 2200 block of Webster Avenue, although somewhat desolate from years of isolation and deterioration, had its own.

What made this particular project so good and bad was that there was limited traffic in the area. If the block was more active, they could never do it, so that was good, but the fact it was so quiet kind of worked against them as well. Anything out of sorts to one of the neighborhood singers could be reported, and things could go south from there.

They had been digging for an hour or so and were growing tired and thirsty. They decided to stop and drink some water next to the abandoned house before continuing. That extra movement caused one of the neighborhood singers to catch notice and place a call unbeknownst to the brothers.

Meanwhile, they were drinking water and taking a break.

"This is my fault fellas," Kolby starts, "I didn't do what I said I would do. Truthfully I could not bring myself to come back up here, period. No excuse though, my word is my bond and I didn't do it."

"Appreciate the apology but I don't know if any of us would've done it. It's not a place mentally where any of us want to be. And me running away when I did and putting it on you was just some cop out shit bruh," Jameson says in response.

"I already apologized so y'all not getting a damn thing out of me now," Eero says. They all smile and chuckle and continue talking.

Meanwhile, the police observed, called for back-up, and gathered to ambush the unusual activity transpiring.

The three of them go back to digging.

One patrol car starts down Bedford, the other down Webster until they come to the same block. They dispatched from their cars and walked until they met where the abandoned house sat. Big Ray is sitting across the street, but he is still asleep. The four officers split up and walked around both sides of the house. As they get to the other side, with guns drawn, they tell everyone to stop.

Fear strikes all of the brothers; one never knows if an officer will pull the trigger. Hard to explain that type of fear, knowing whatever good or bad intentions you have, your last breath could come after hearing from an officer of the law.

They all immediately stop and fall to their knees with hands behind their heads. Thankfully and to some degree, expectedly, these officers are more curious than anything. As they sit there, Kolby quietly says, "Don't say anything, no matter what they say. Paul Romano is our lawyer, we will only speak to him... You hear me?"

"Yeah," Eero and Kolby say simultaneously.

So much for going back home tonight.

44

The Ghosts That Keep Me Awake

The brothers are detained and questioned. They say nothing; they all ask for Mr. Paul Romano, who picks them up and brings them to his office. It's late now, around 2 a.m., they are exhausted, irritated, and feel defeated. Each of them speaks to Mr. Romano.

Mr. Romano sits and hands Eero a cup of coffee, "I need to know what's up. I can't help you all if I don't get the full story, help me out please?"

Eero sits for a moment and reluctantly starts, "Every neighborhood has their special wino, sometimes if you live in a neighborhood like ours, each block or two had their own special wino. They are kind of like mascots, you watch them stumble home and laugh at them, almost on a nightly basis. The amazing thing is these guys live forever, they don't die from bad livers or any of that shit.

Our block the wino was Crazy Eddie. All of our lives we had seen him, literally since I was five years old I can recount seeing this fool drink, stumble home, and repeat the same thing every day for years. As we grew older we began to notice he picked on Kolby more than anybody, he would talk shit to him, Kolby would throw it right back at him. That all makes sense now but at the time we paid no attention to it, and Kolby never said anything so we just continued on."

"Jameson, why was Crazy Eddie someone you all attempted to avoid?" Mr. Romano asks Jameson.

Jameson says, "Crazy Eddie was not your typical wino. He didn't just drink, he also liked little boys. Kolby was always a little bit more hip to the game than us, his mother would tell him shit that we probably didn't need to know but she felt she had to tell because he was an only child. That's the reason we would scatter home so quickly when the lights came on... was because Eddie would try to catch someone, we never knew what he would do but the last thing you wanted was to try and find out.

Occasionally I would see him but a quick zig zag and his drunk ass would fall out before you would have to worry about him laying a finger on you. As we grew older, we could stay out later. We didn't have to run in when the street lights came on, so we would be out later. And in the summer when the sun goes down later, we would be out until it was nightfall."

Jameson continues, "One particular night when we're about 12 or so we run home. Kolby has the longest run by about a block or so. My phone rang and my mother asked me where Kolby was, I told her he ran home like we all did. Long story short, the next morning Kolby was quiet, he was barely talking. We played ball that day, ran to Ozanam and played games, but all day he's basically silent. Kolby was never quiet, never. So Eero and I pulled him to the side."

"Kolby, what did you tell Eero and Jameson when they pulled you aside?" asks Mr. Romano.

Unlike his usual tenacious self, Kolby was very uncomfortable at this point, "I told Eero and Jameson what happened. I didn't run home like usual, I walked, I turned on my block and this muthafucka grabs my arm."

Mr. Romano asks, "Was that Crazy Eddie?"

"Yeah," Kolby answers.

Mr. Romano sensing Kolby's uneasiness, stops for a moment and sips his water. Kolby looks down and closes his eyes for a moment. Mr. Romano continues, "I hate to ask this but did he rape you Kolby?"

Kolby does not respond; he glances outside of the window into the dark night. That night changed him forever, he vowed never to be a victim of anything again, but he never forgave himself for being a vulnerable boy taken advantage of by a menace. For the first time in over two decades, he had to recount that night fully—the terror, pain, and humiliation he felt. It made his entire body go numb; he began sweating, his stomach dropped to the floor, he felt helpless and vulnerable once again. Tears slowly rolling down his face, Kolby says, "He did enough to me that twenty plus years later, I can still feel how I felt that night." Kolby gets up and leaves the room.

Mr. Romano says, "Eero, what happened after Kolby told you what happened to him?"

Eero responds, "After he told us that, it was my idea to kill that fucking asshole. There was no way we'd run from him ever again, period. So that weekend, we set up a scheme; we asked to stay at Kolby's because his mother would always go out on Friday evenings around 10 p.m. We knew Eddie would sleep in that abandoned house typically, I grabbed some hammers, a couple of shovels, and we went up there and beat his ass to death."

Eero continues, "Then we buried him, 10 steps out and five to the right. Because he was dead by 10:15 p.m. and that was the only thing that could make it right, was to end his life."

Mr. Romano asks, "Why didn't you just tell your parents or the police Jameson?"

Jameson responds, "Nah, this had to be this way, nobody in our neighborhood goes to their parents with a story like that and definitely not the police. We just handled it ourselves, that's the only way we could give our boy justice, not leaving it up to anyone else."

"I understand, you all get some rest," Mr. Romano says, "I think I know what we need to do. This might require telling this story to the public, before they dig that body up, and find the necklace."

45

Day of Reckoning

ameson and Ryann are sitting in his Audi outside of the Pittsburgh Police headquarters on Western Avenue. Mr. Romano had made arrangements for each of the brothers to turn themselves in for questioning and make everything official.

The last couple of weeks have been a blur for Jameson; everything else seemed relatively unimportant after such an emotionally charged event. He did not trust the system and was petrified that he could lose all he worked for regardless of how justifiable it was in his mind.

"Do you know if anyone else is here yet?" Ryann asks.

"Nope, haven't reached out to anyone, we all know what we need to do."

"I'm really sorry Jameson... I'm sorry for what you had to do and for now, I just wish I could help," Ryann says as she begins to tear up.

Jameson gently wipes her tears away.

"Don't cry, I don't trust the system but I think we'll be fine. I'm more worried about Z and you. I don't want this to blow up and have to deal with Camryn from inside."

"You can't worry about that right now, Paul has helped us out with that. I don't think you'll be in here long, hopefully this goes away quickly."

"All my life this I've steered clear of the law. Biggie said it best, either you slang crack rock or you got a wicked jump shot. I never really played ball, but metaphorically I used my mind to steer clear of the streets. And now look at me, I have everything, and it can be taken away even if it's temporarily by someone else. Makes me feel like this was all a waste," Jameson says defeatedly.

"No, not at all. And you can't have that negative mindset... You, no... *we* can't have that negative mindset. We have unfinished business, you need to be here for Zanita, we need to make us official, make a family and all take care of one another."

Jameson smiles and nods in agreement.

"You know I love you," Ryann says defiantly.

"I love you too."

They hug one another and kiss.

Jameson still loves how she smells, how she smiles at him every time they see one another, and for loving him like no one he has ever met. But, unfortunately, men can sometimes be fools and not realize what they have until it's too late. He is thankful he was given a second chance with Ryann. But right now, his biggest battle was about to take place.

Jameson takes a deep breath, places his face in his hands, and exhales while closing his eyes. He looks outside, and today is a clear, cool autumn day, partly cloudy like always. The birds are chirping as they fly about freely; the trees are beginning to lose their leaves and change colors. The fall was always his favorite season; he hoped he would enjoy it from the outside.

He steps outside the car, the cool air hits his face, and he walks into the building, ready to face what comes his way.

~ The End ~

About the Author

J.C. Benson was never one to take the traditional route. Even as a kid growing up in Pittsburgh, Pennsylvania, he was an outlier and unique. As many youth growing up in the inner city, he gravitated towards sports and eventually earned a full scholarship playing college basketball. Along the way though, he would always gravitate towards another love of his, storytelling. Rather it be short stories, poetry or the like he would express his thoughts and feelings with a pen on paper.

After graduating from college, he would go on to start a film production company. The company, Fear No Man Productions would go on to produce several short films, two feature films and other productions as well. His work did well in film festivals and received many accolades yet never took off as he envisioned.

After over a decade of hiatus from storytelling he is back and full of vigor and ready to show the world his talents. The new vision is simple yet complex, *Storytelling for our Culture*. There are many stories to tell in many different mediums and J.C. Benson is poised and ready for the journey.

Follow J.C. Benson

FB: J.C. Benson

IG: @j.c.benson3

Twitter: @Jeff_BensonJr

jcbenson.com

"Work without permission."

- Ava DuVernay